For the daughters of the daughters of the daughters
and the sons of the sons of the sons,
when this story has been not just forgotten
but wiped out.
—Ricardo Chávez Castañeda

For María, my daughter.
—Alejandro Magallanes

About Unruly

This is the third book to be published under Unruly, Enchanted Lion's new imprint of picture books for teenagers and adults. We launched Unruly because we believe that we never age out of pictures and visual stories and that we long for them across our lives.

This illustrated work is a ghost story, a horror story, and a work of literary fiction.

THE BOOK OF DENIAL

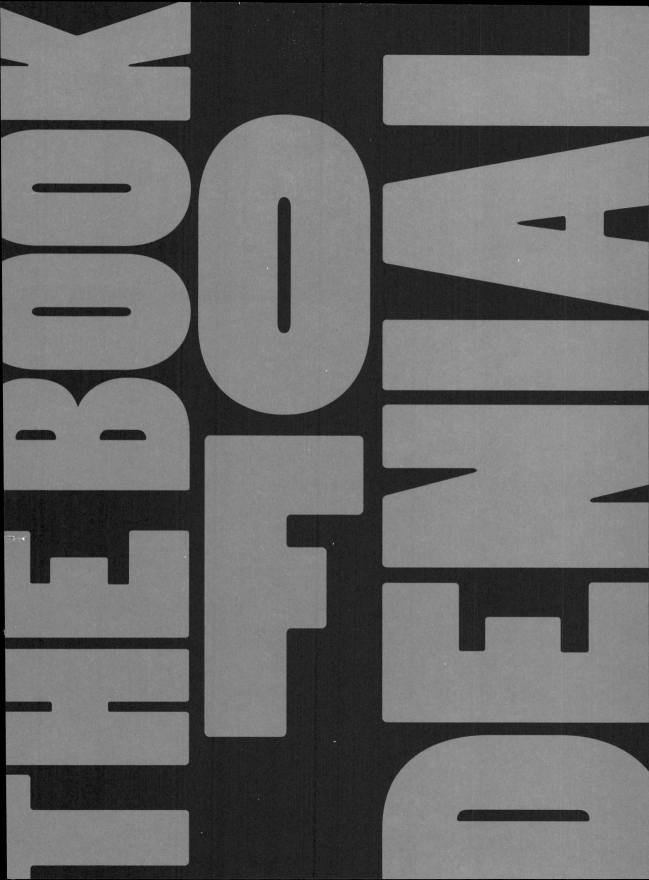

www.enchantedlion.com

First English-language edition published in 2024 by Enchanted Lion Books,
248 Creamer Street, Studio 4, Brooklyn, NY 11231
Original Spanish-language edition copyright © 2014 by
Ediciones El Naranjo, S.A. de C.V., Mexico
Text copyright © 2014 by Ricardo Chávez Castañeda
Illustrations copyright © 2014 by Alejandro Magallanes
English-language translation copyright © 2024 by Lawrence Schimel

Design adaptation for the English-language edition by Jazmin Miralles

Six images come from the work of Gustave Doré, Giovanni Pisano,
Michael Wolgemut, and Peter Paul Rubens

All rights reserved under International and
Pan-American Copyright Conventions
A CIP record is on file with the Library of Congress
ISBN 978-1-59270-362-3
Printed in China by RR Donnelley Asia Printing Solutions Ltd.

First Printing

THE BOOK OF DENIAL

Written by Ricardo Chávez Castañeda

Translated from Spanish by Lawrence Schimel

Illustration and design by Alejandro Magallanes

an
Enchanted Lion Book
NEW YORK

PROLOGUE

This story
is the worst story
in the world.

It's absolutely terrible.

For those who don't like tragic stories,
this book has a happy ending
on a page near the end.

I recommend you
stop reading after that.

My mother always told me that some books are not for children.

I didn't understand what she meant until yesterday, when I secretly read the book my father is writing.

It's called *The Book of Denial*... but I didn't start reading it because of its title.

Mamá was in bed. Papá was sitting beside her, as he does so often now, and I was going down the hallway when I heard him tell her, "The children need to know."

"The children need to know this story of terror," he whispered, leaning forward as if to kiss her.

This made me want to read his book, because he hasn't written anything for almost a year.

Not a single word, even though the books he has written fill almost a whole shelf in his library.

How does he have so many ideas in his head? I've often wondered about this, while running my fingers along the spines of the dozens of books of his that have been published.

On each spine, his name is written in a bright color with gilt edges.

That's my father, I'm amazed to think, staring at his last name, which is also my own.

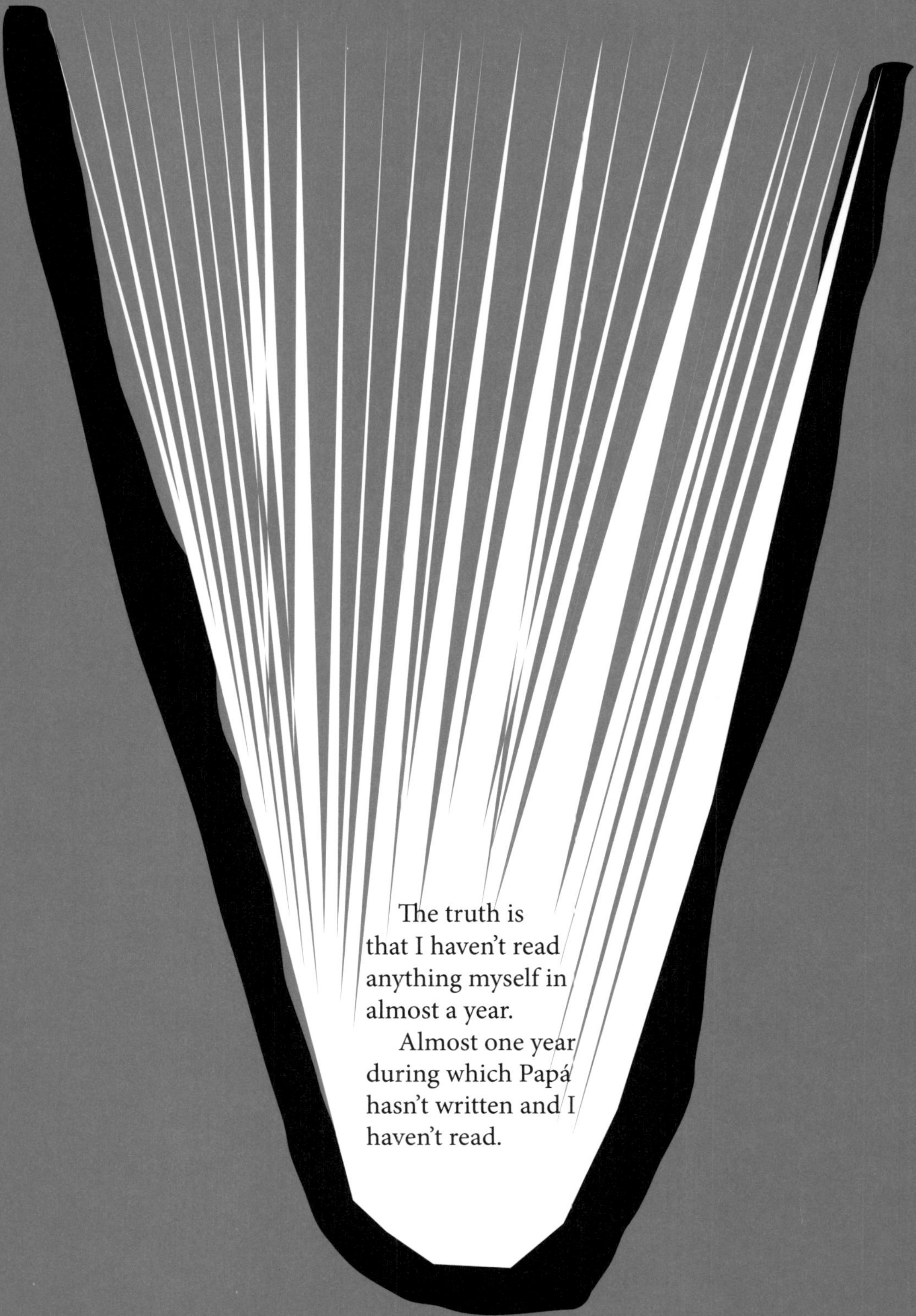

The truth is that I haven't read anything myself in almost a year.

Almost one year during which Papá hasn't written and I haven't read.

The only one of us who sometimes reads is Mamá. She leans back in bed and unfolds the letter she keeps in her drawer. Her eyes move slowly over the page, as if they were falling and rising, falling and rising.

"The children need to know this story of terror." That's what Papá told her that night. Perhaps he had forgotten that I had already read many tales of terror—about monsters, the dead, ghosts, haunted houses, and staircases leading down, down, down into the center of the earth. *Why would I need to hear a new horror story?*

I guess horror and candy
work in the exact same way.
You forget that the taste of
sweetness exists, until suddenly
there's a knock at the door and a
little girl selling cookies appears.
Overhearing my father that night
made me want to go into his study
to see the book he was writing,
because I had forgotten that
horror stories exist.

(*Just a glance.*)

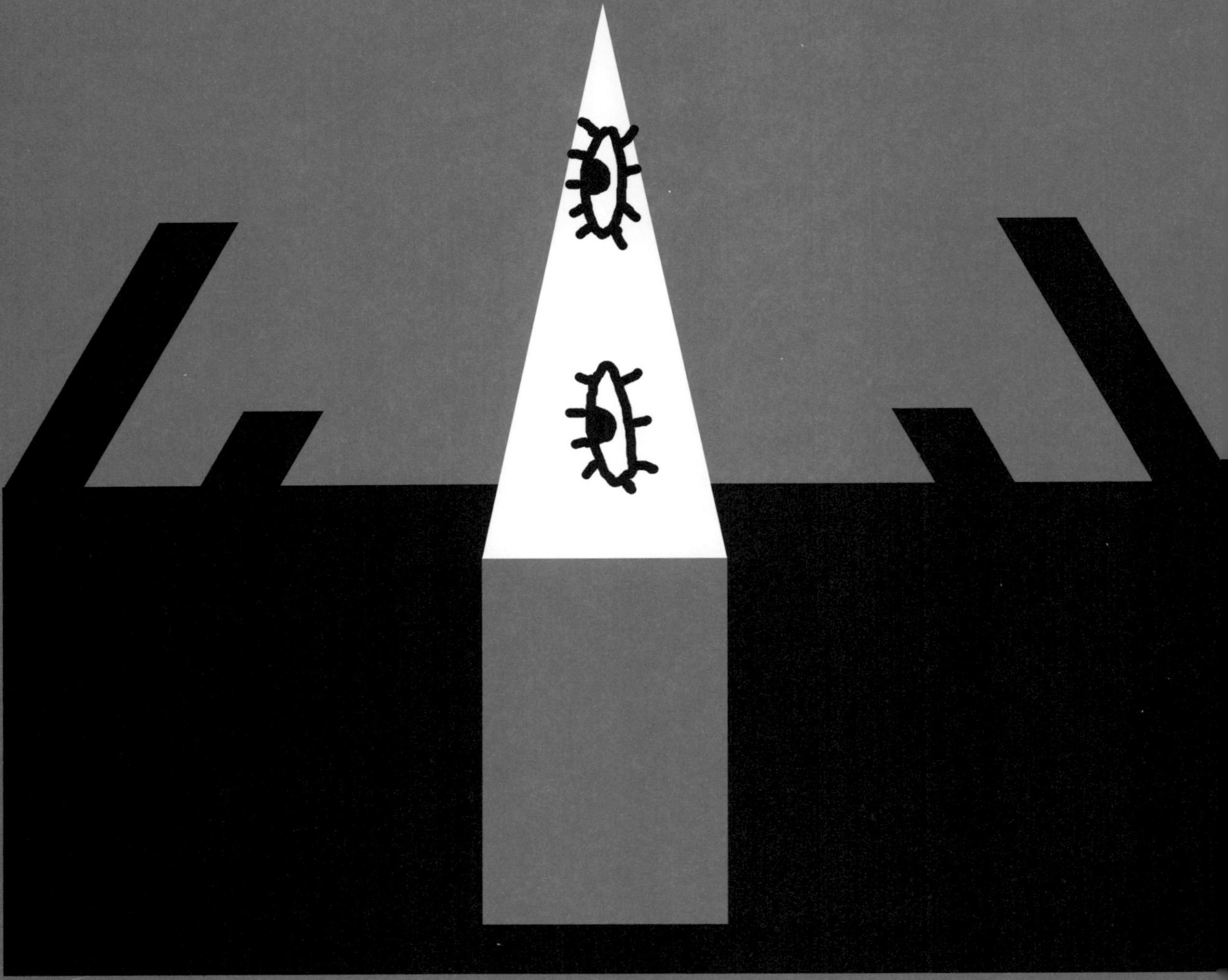

My father's study is very dark, very quiet, and very serious, like an angry face with just one eye, which is his leather chair, and a line mouth, which is his desk of dark wood. The desk is now covered with dust, because my father doesn't like anyone to go in there. Up until a few days ago, emptiness had also settled over the desk, because he had forgotten to set out a hardcover notebook like the one I found there last night.

I'm just going to take a peek,

I thought again.

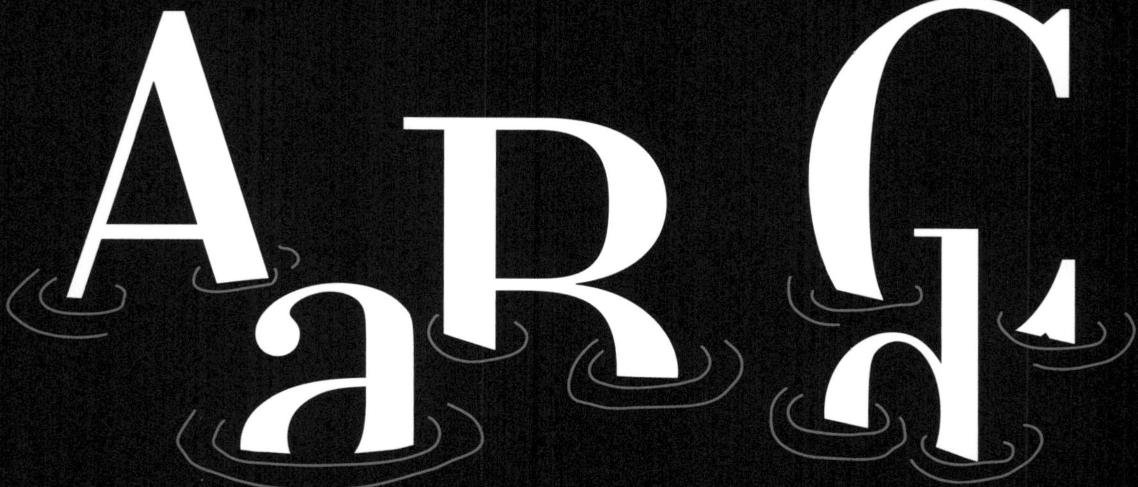

How can you see letters without
wanting to read them?
How can you look at the sea without
wanting to swim in it?

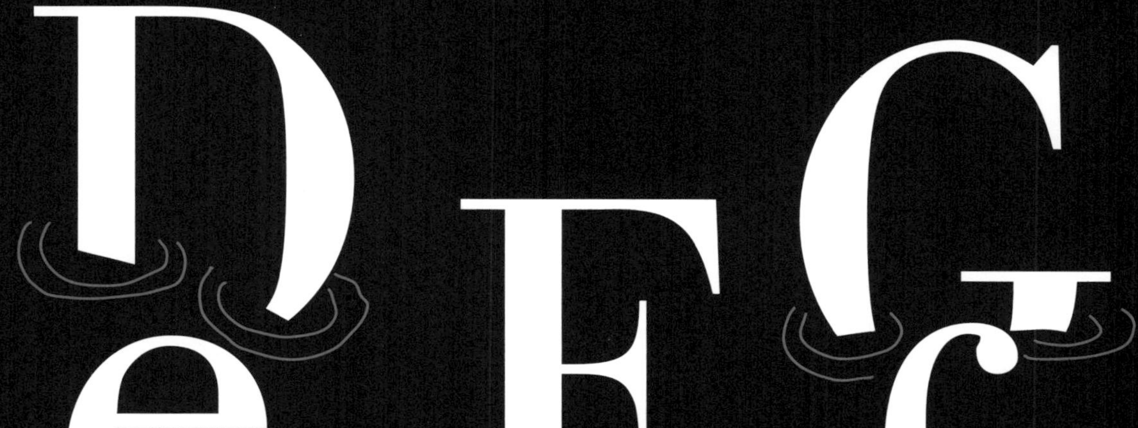

I didn't read everything that Papá had written. I couldn't even make it through a single page.

I went up to his desk and opened the notebook at random. It had a hard cover, and its pages were completely blank—unlined and marginless, just as he prefers for jotting down his ideas.

"Give me a page without a prison," he always says. "Free of vertical and horizontal bars, to think whatever is necessary."

The passage I read that night was written in his beautiful handwriting, which looks as if it's tilted by the wind and undulating like waves. A white sea of wave upon wave, moving across the page like a strong ocean current.

It's in this sea that I began to swim, although I had sworn that I wouldn't read a word of it until he had given me permission.

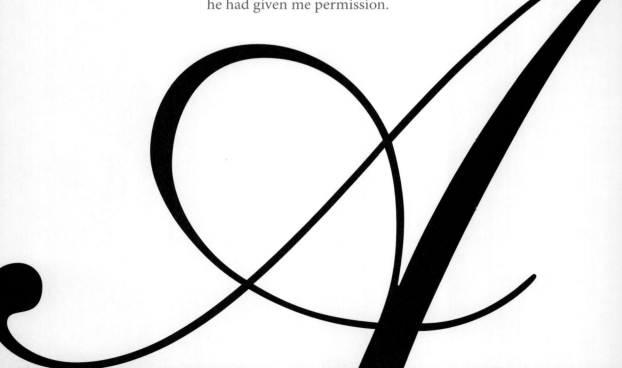

The hand of an adult is the size of a child's face, so the executioners of children need no weapons. The children are made to face away from them, and the executioners approach from behind. All they have to do is place their hands over the children's faces, as if covering them with a scarf, gently protecting their little mouths and faces from the cold. Then, the executioners need only press down with their hands, until the children are suffocated.

I stopped reading, feeling as if I were the one who was suffocating.

When I went back to bed, I realized

that I no longer liked horror stories.

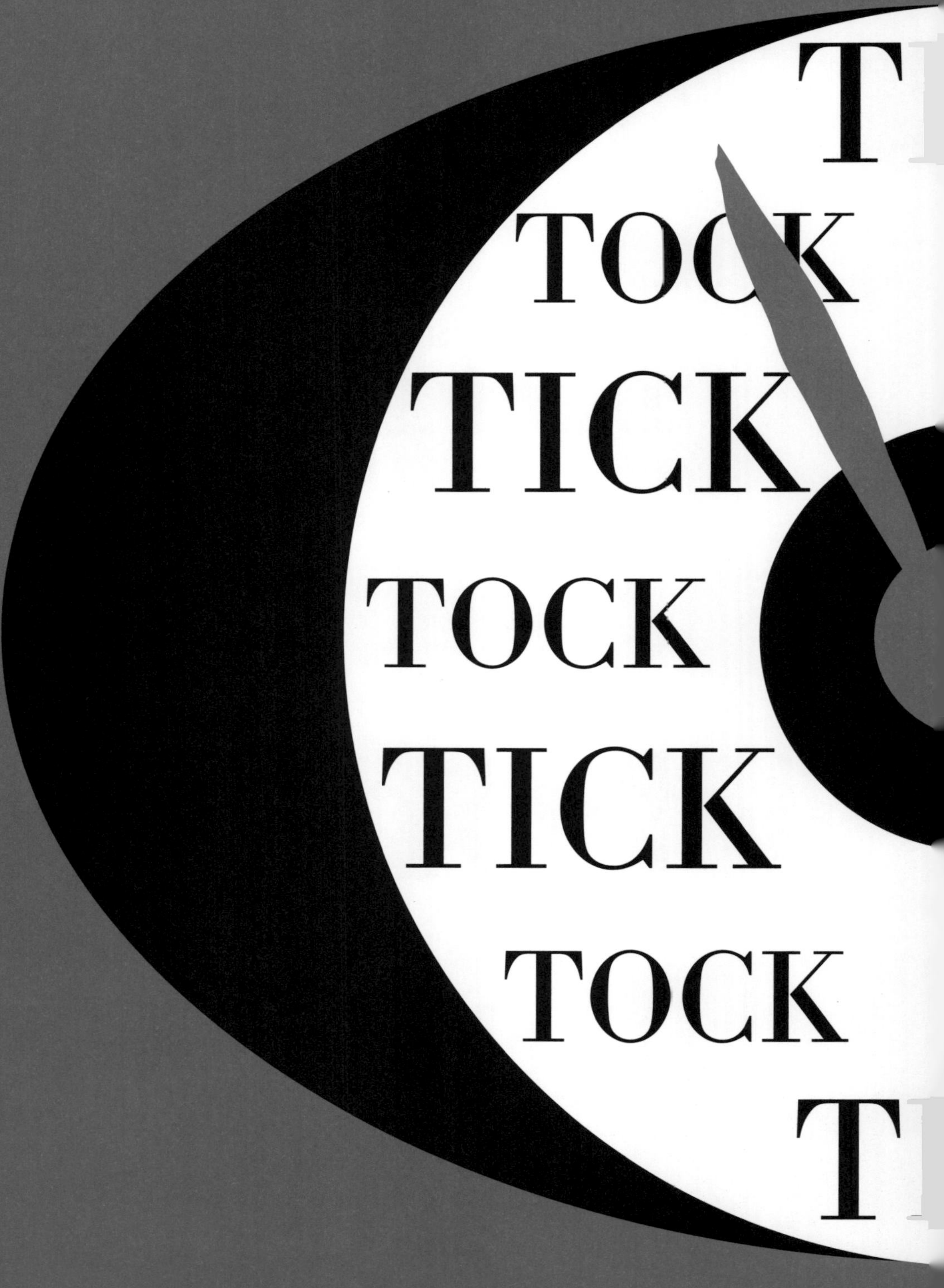
T
TOCK
TICK
TOCK
TICK
TOCK
T

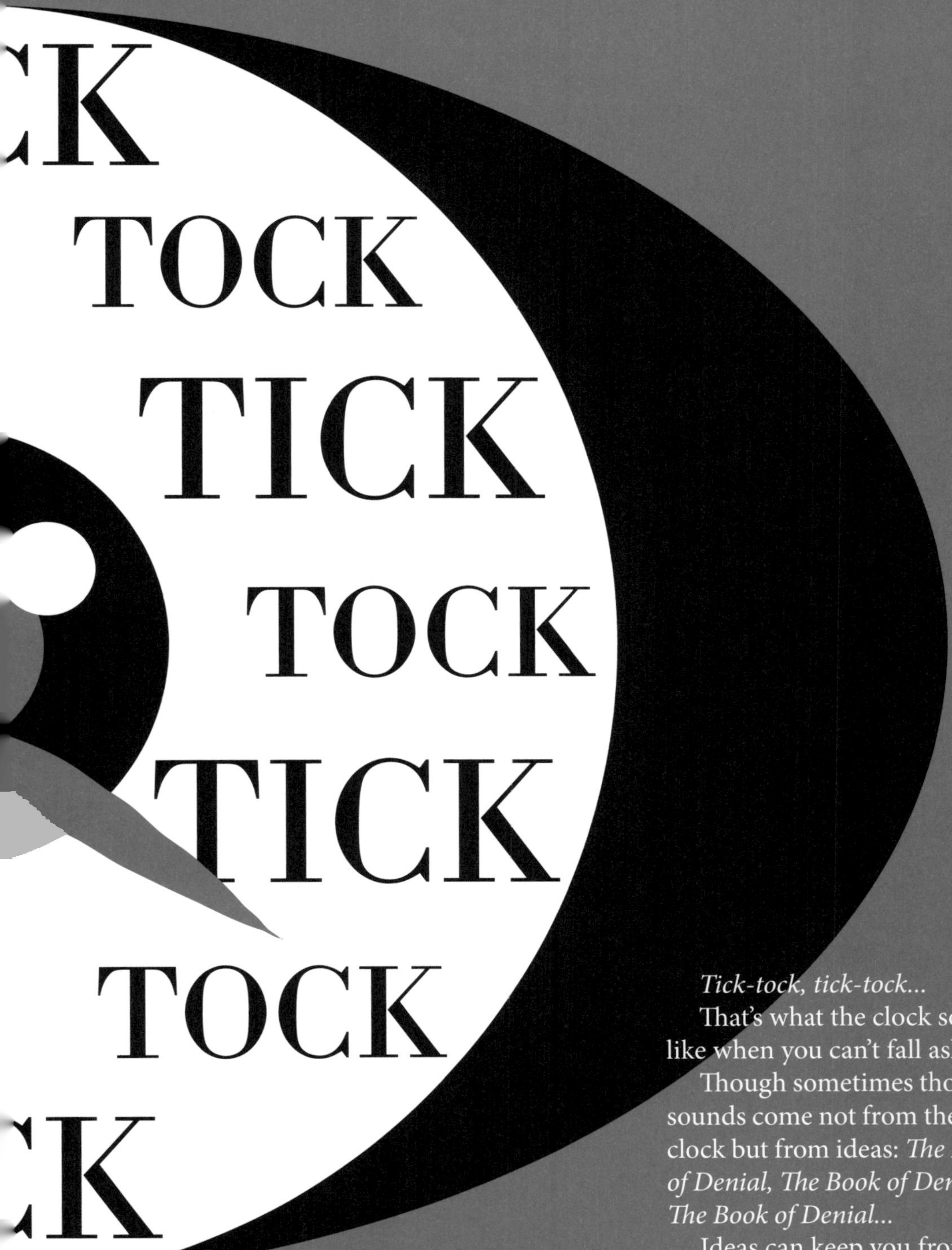
TOCK
TICK
TOCK
TICK
TOCK

Tick-tock, tick-tock...

That's what the clock sounds like when you can't fall asleep.

Though sometimes those sounds come not from the clock but from ideas: *The Book of Denial, The Book of Denial, The Book of Denial...*

Ideas can keep you from sleeping, too.

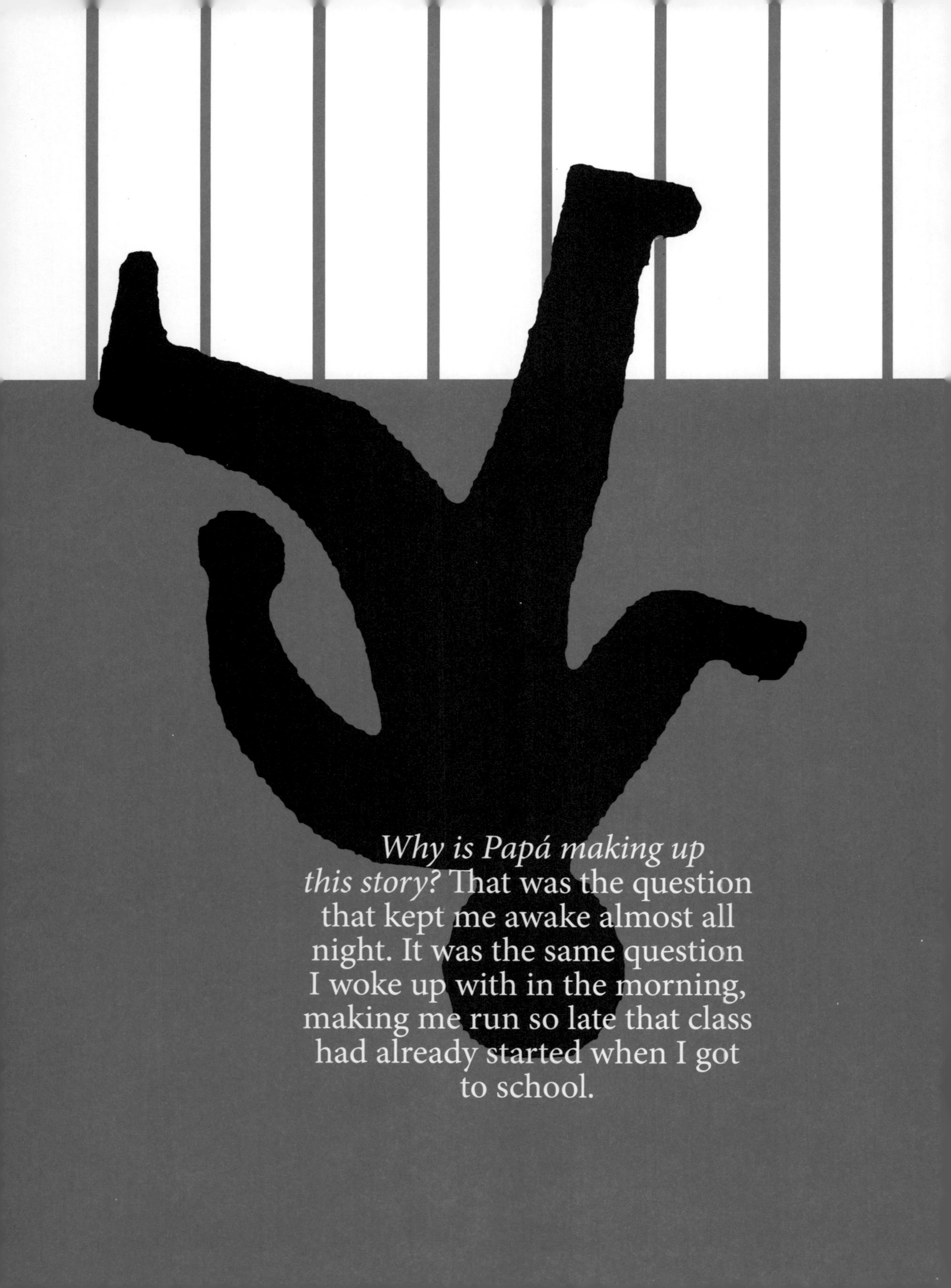

Why is Papá making up this story? That was the question that kept me awake almost all night. It was the same question I woke up with in the morning, making me run so late that class had already started when I got to school.

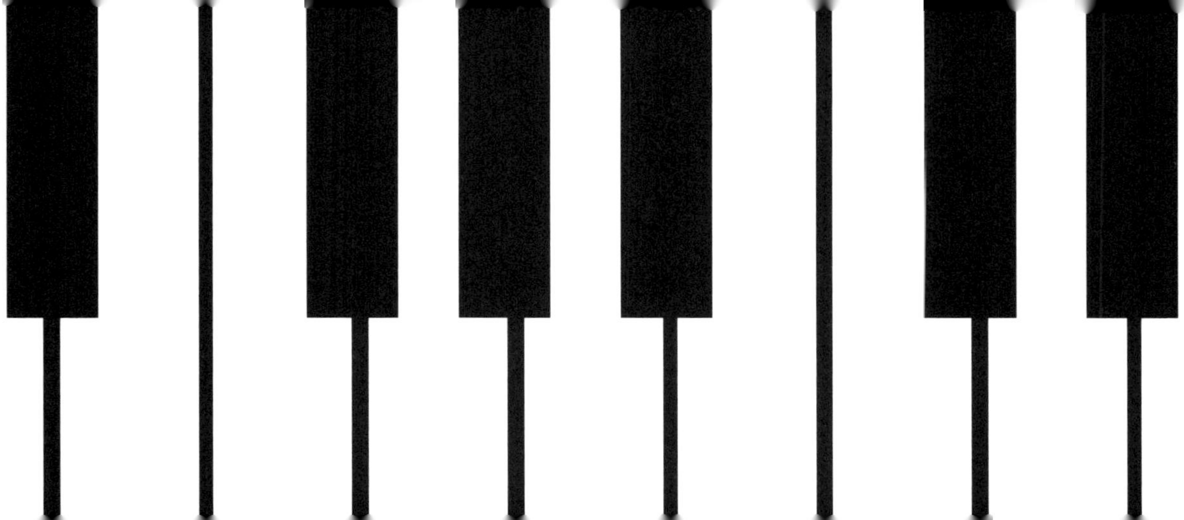

When I got home, Mamá had already set the table with three plates, three napkins, and three sets of silverware, but I couldn't sit down.

The truth is that I read more than one page last night.

It has always been easy for humankind to get rid of its children. The necks of children are still fragile, they are like weak paper cones, each balacing an enormous crystal ball.

It's as if nature itself were on our side, the side of the adults.

It's so easy to wring their fragile necks, or to snap them like kindling. That's what it sounds like, according to the few who have dared to speak of this: "Like breaking apart a rotten table."

Suddenly, I was afraid
of seeing my father's hands.

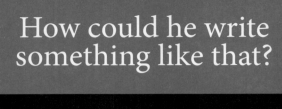
How could he write something like that?

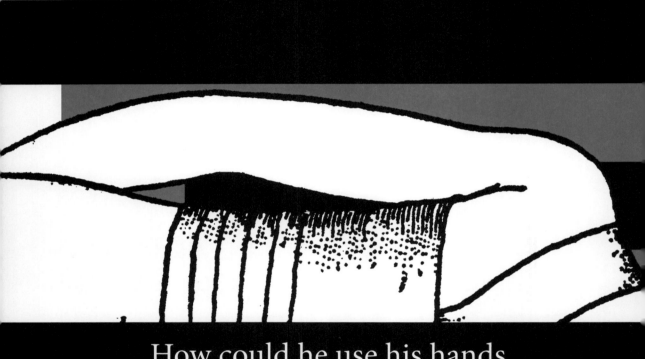
How could he use his hands to write something like that?

I stayed at the top of the staircase
looking between the banisters.

Throughout lunch, while Mamá ate,
Papá remained hunched over, his body
leaning forward, his hands under the table.

Maybe he couldn't bring himself
to look at his hands, either...

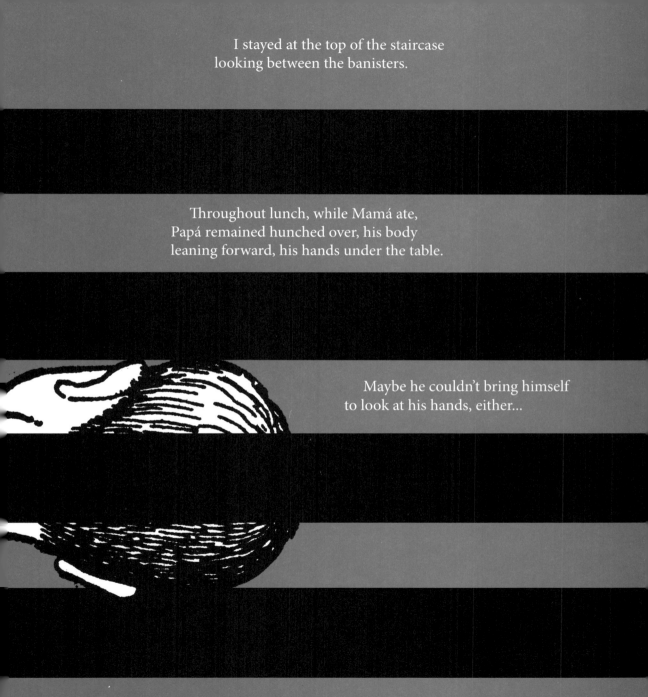

"I need to write it so that others will care," my father said.

He was sitting on the bed again, my mother was lying down again, and I was outside the half-open door of their bedroom just like before.

This time, my presence there was not accidental. I had gone there specifically to see them without their seeing me.

My mother was under the blankets and had her eyes closed; Papá had his eyes closed, as well.

"Do you think it's easy to do something like this? Do you think I do this because I like it?" he asked her without looking at her, rocking back and forth. "I write so that others will care, but also so that it continues to matter to me... I must do it while I still care, darling, I must do it while it still matters to me."

After, Papá went to the kitchen, the living room, the kitchen, the dining room, the kitchen, the garden, the living room...

   He didn't actually do anything in those rooms. He just stood there, looking at the furniture, the photographs on the wall, and the rugs.

   Finally, he sat down, and I hid behind his chair. The last thing I thought before falling asleep was that he was acting just like I did whenever I had homework due for school: keeping myself busy with anything else, so as not to do what I had to do.

"There is no longer path than the one that leads to obligation," Mamá once told me. "So let me help you." And she brought me my schoolbooks so I could do my homework.

I'm not going to help you. That was the first thing I thought this morning when I woke up, no longer behind the chair where I had fallen asleep, but tucked into my bed. *I promise you, Papá.*

In class today, the teacher talked to us about the world, about the body, about numbers... But it all went in one ear and out the other until she spoke of history, of one of the chapters of human history: the Holy Innocents.

Afterwards, I couldn't even stand up from my desk to go to recess.

How did she know?

This was the only question that echoed inside of my head and across the silent classroom. The idea was like the ringing of a bell, growing more and more deafening with each peal. *How did my teacher find out about the story that Papá wrote?*

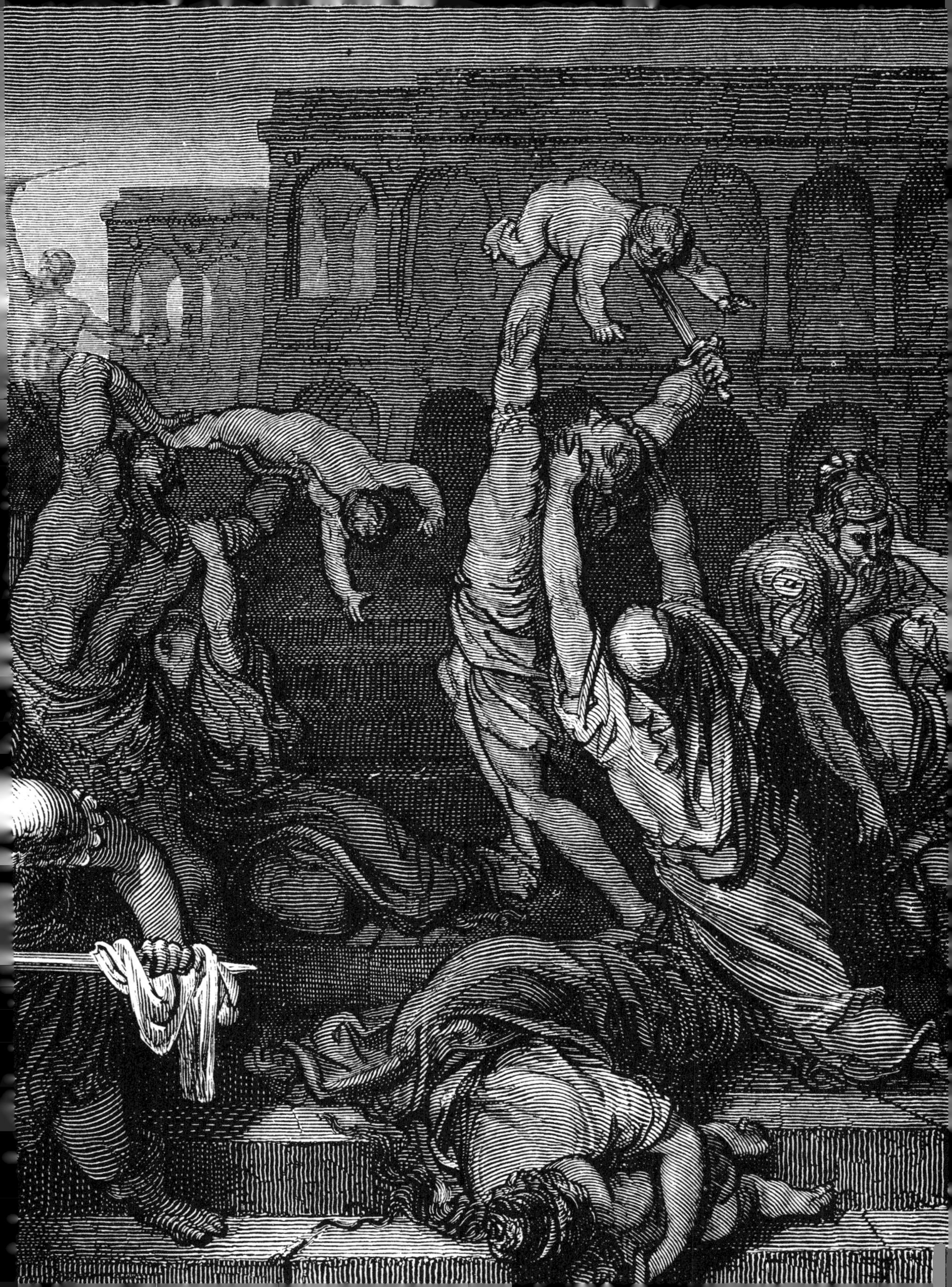

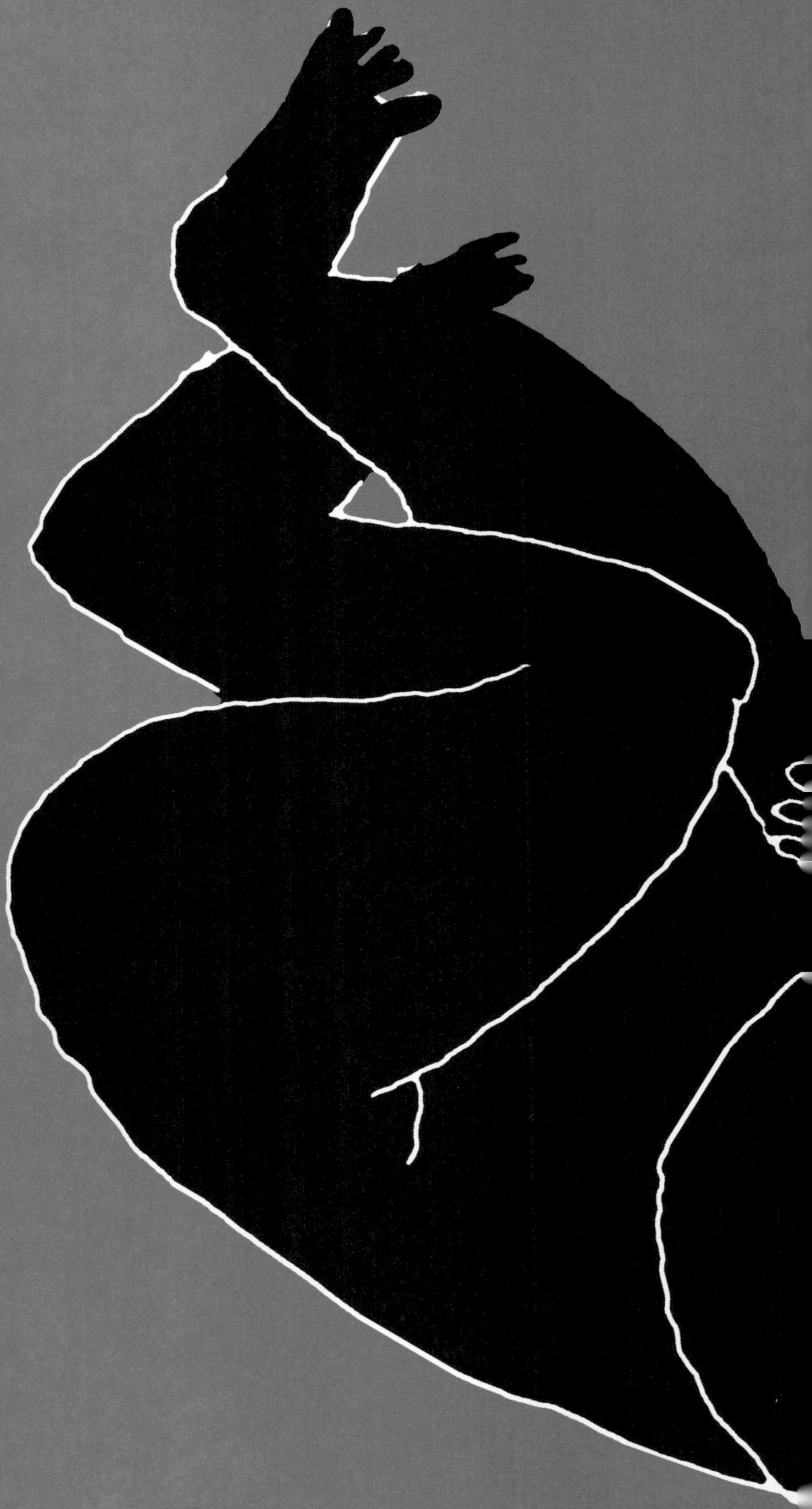

In *The Book of Denial*, he wrote:

We've always imagined that weapons were involved. But it need not have been knives or swords, for almost anything can be a weapon if the goal is to kill a child. Our imagination shows us the terrible night of the Holy Innocents with hundreds of men brandishing sharpened and bloodied weapons. But in reality, it's more believable to think that these men scoured the streets—kicking open the doors of homes, searching under the furniture, inside chests, behind the clothes, any place where a child under two could be hidden—and seized any infant they found with their two bare hands. And with those same naked hands, they put an end to them without any bloody spectacle. They exterminated those infants in the most macabre fashion. That is to say, without distance. Without separating the one who kills from the one being killed, as any weapon forces us to do. Without the distance of a lance, without the distance of a sword, without even the minimal distance a knife imposes... They murdered them at the nonexistent distance of any act of love.

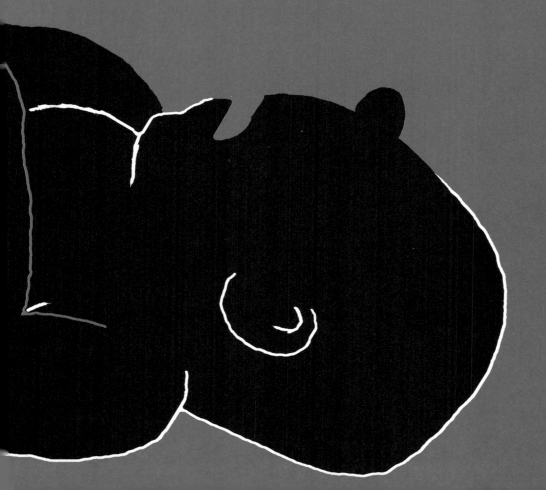

Suddenly, I remembered going to school for the first time.

Until then, I had thought that school didn't exist, that it was a lie invented by my parents to frighten me when I misbehaved. I thought they'd bribed all the children I saw through my bedroom window with candy, some fruit, or a bit of money so they would dress in uniform and lug backpacks in front of me.

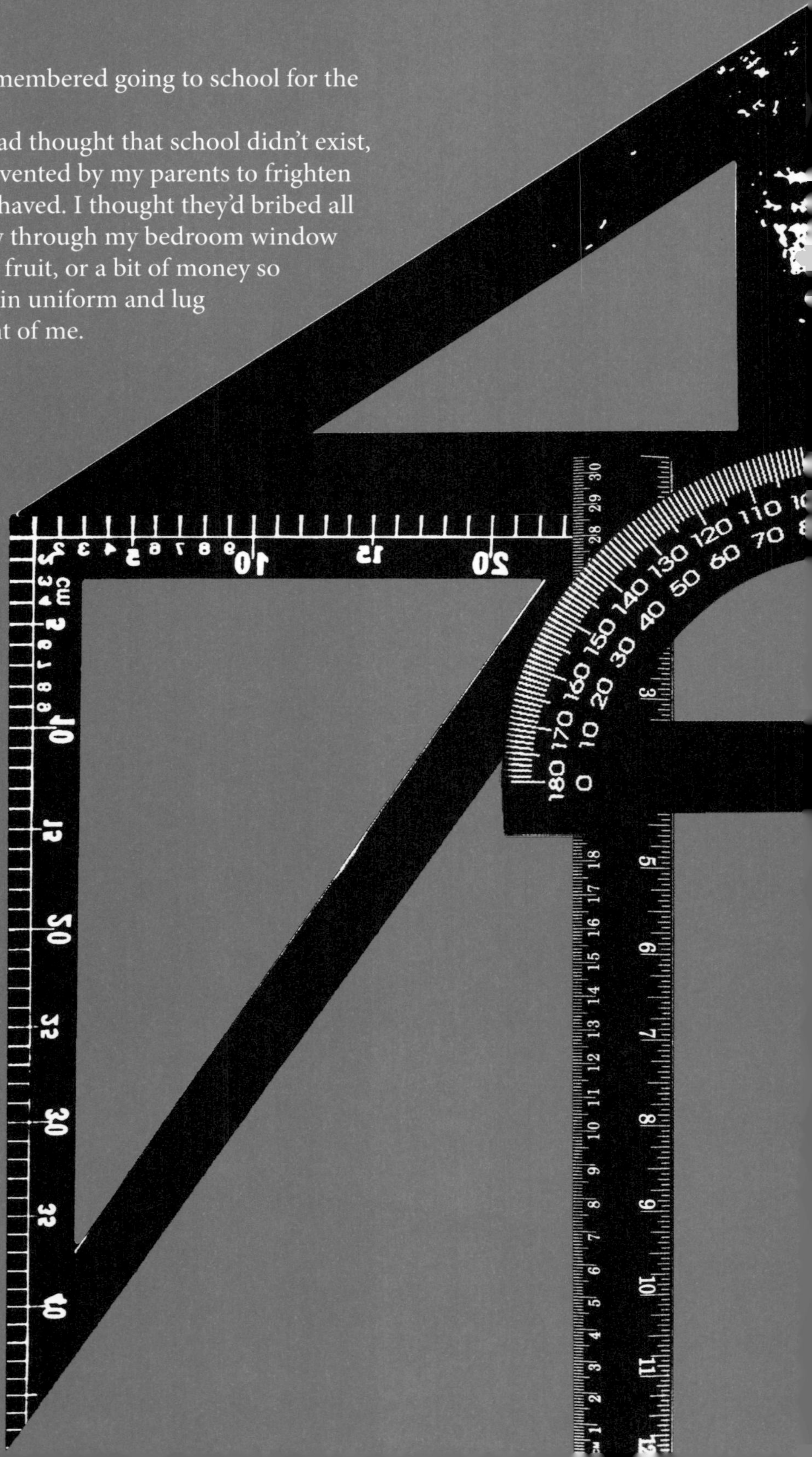

I remember the moment when, hand in hand with Mamá and Papá, I wound up in front of an enormous building with an enormous sign in enormous letters.

I didn't know how to read, but I stopped and stood there, making a real effort to understand those black stripes on that enormous building's enormous sign.

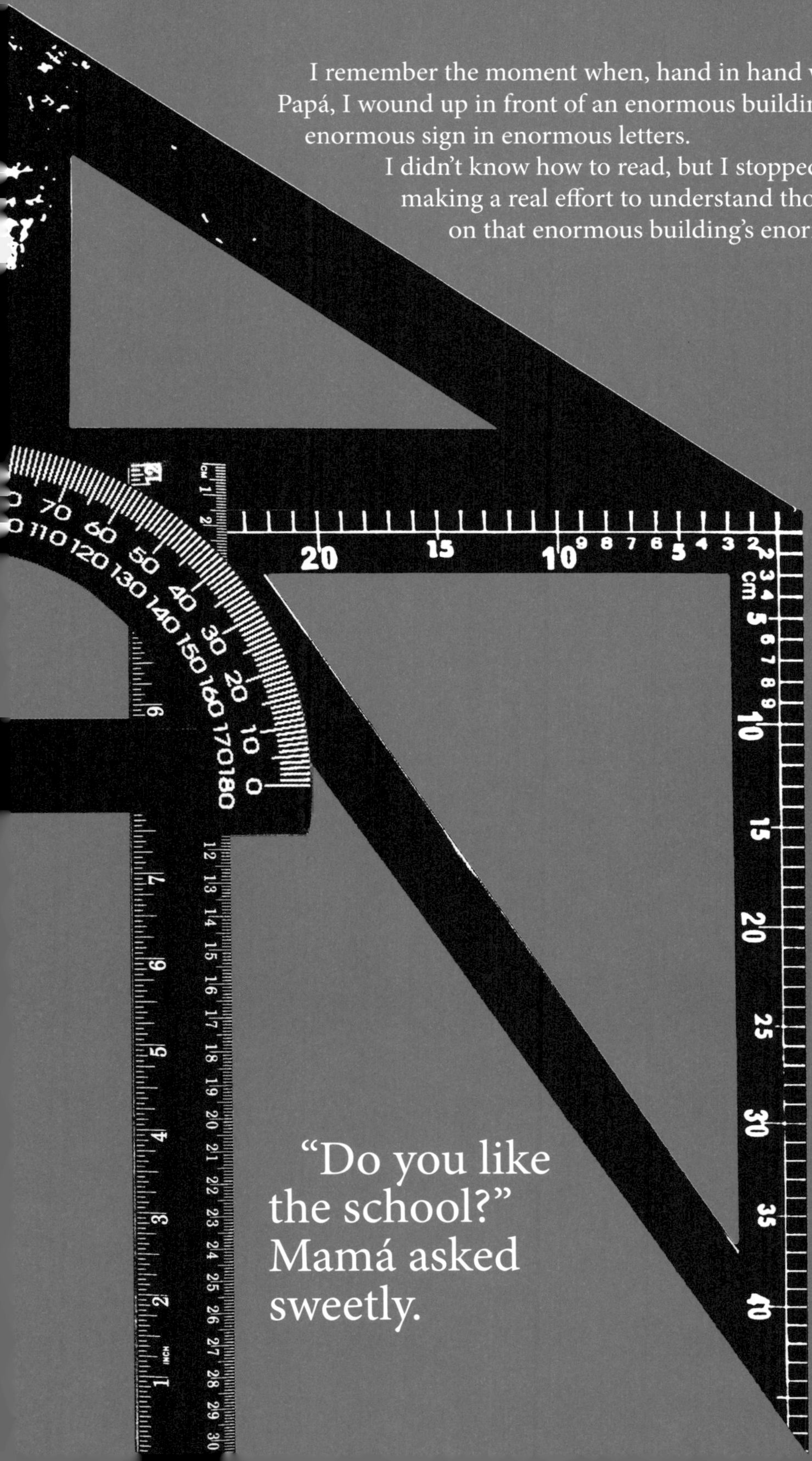

"Do you like the school?" Mamá asked sweetly.

It was as if my teacher had asked us something similar after she finished telling us the story of the Holy Innocents in that classroom. **"Do you like the world in which you live?"**

I looked at my classmates and immediately knew that none of them had read Papá's book, and therefore none of them had known the story until just then.

They were all very serious, very still, and very pale.

María, a girl with glasses, freckles, and braids, who would always sit up front, raised her hand.

"Yes, María?" the teacher asked.

"What did the mamás and papás do?" she asked, in a voice that was so quiet it could barely be heard at the back of the classroom.

I felt just like I had felt the first time I saw the school sign. Back then, I didn't know how to read—and so I couldn't figure out if my parents' joke was really a joke or not. But now, precisely because I can read, I keep on seeing the Holy Innocents mentioned everywhere I look. Now that I'm back home, they're in every encyclopedia, every one of my father's history books, even on the calendar hanging on the refrigerator.

Sometimes, it's impossible to do something as simple as turning an inside-out glove back the right way.

How is it that so many people already know the story that Papá has only started to write? That was the question I couldn't get out of my head, until I accidentally turned it right-side out.

Why was Papá writing about something that everyone already knew?

Well, that almost everyone knew.

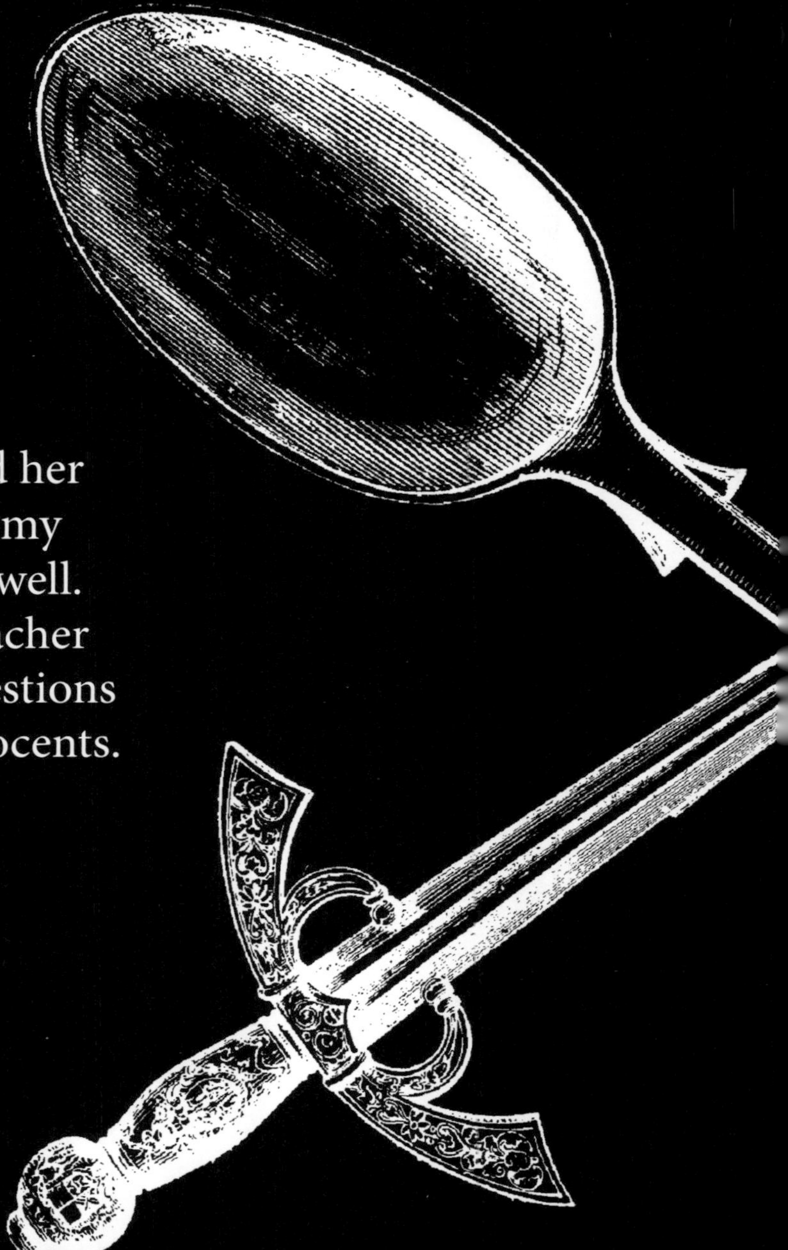

After María raised her hand, the rest of my classmates did as well. They asked the teacher more and more questions about the Holy Innocents.

Some of the questions were: "How can someone run away when they haven't even learned to walk yet?"

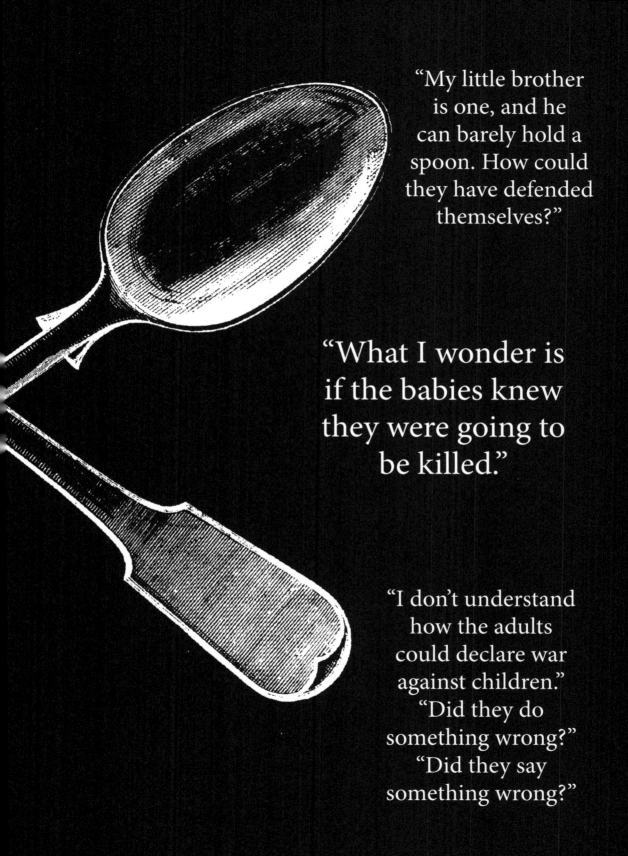

"My little brother is one, and he can barely hold a spoon. How could they have defended themselves?"

"What I wonder is if the babies knew they were going to be killed."

"I don't understand how the adults could declare war against children."
"Did they do something wrong?"
"Did they say something wrong?"

What I would ask my teacher now is: Why did she tell us that story?

And I would also ask her: Why had no one told it to us before?

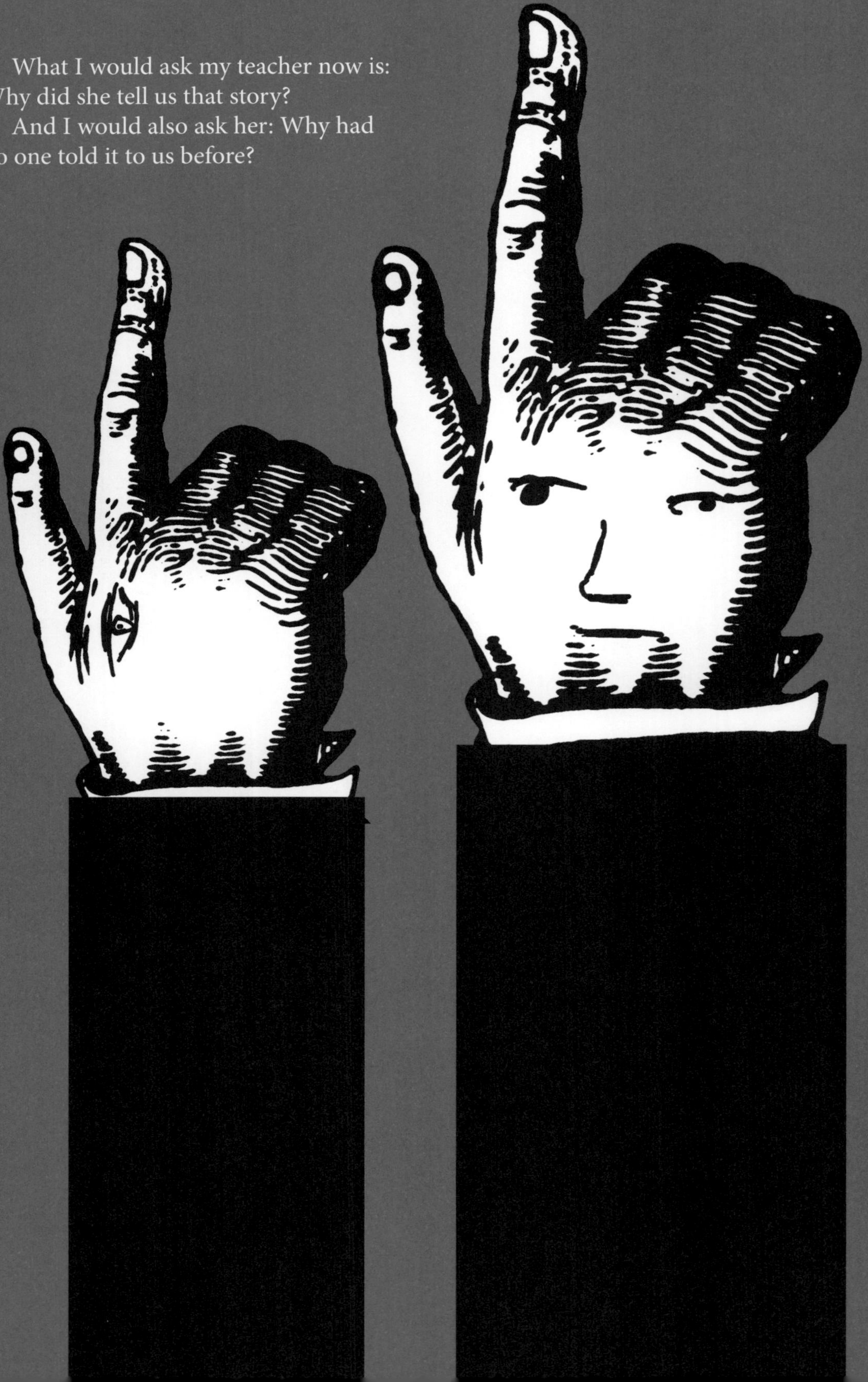

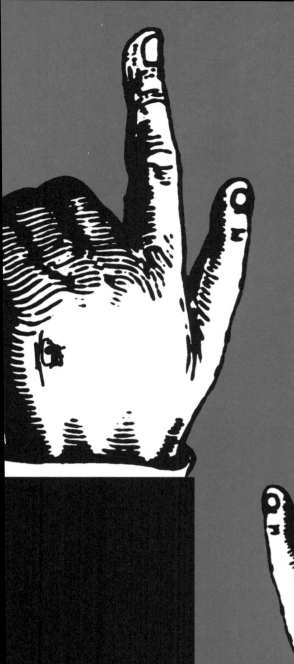

That night, I had a dream. Papá appeared in the classroom with his hardcover notebook, and he asked us if we wanted to listen to a story.

"Raise your hand if you want to hear a story," he said.

When all of my classmates started to raise their hands, I ran from desk to desk lowering their arms, until my own shouts woke me up, crying for María to please help me.

“Help me!”

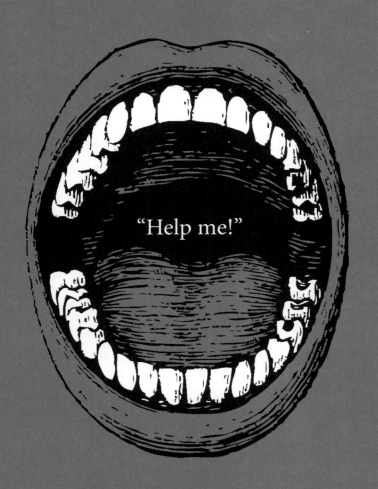

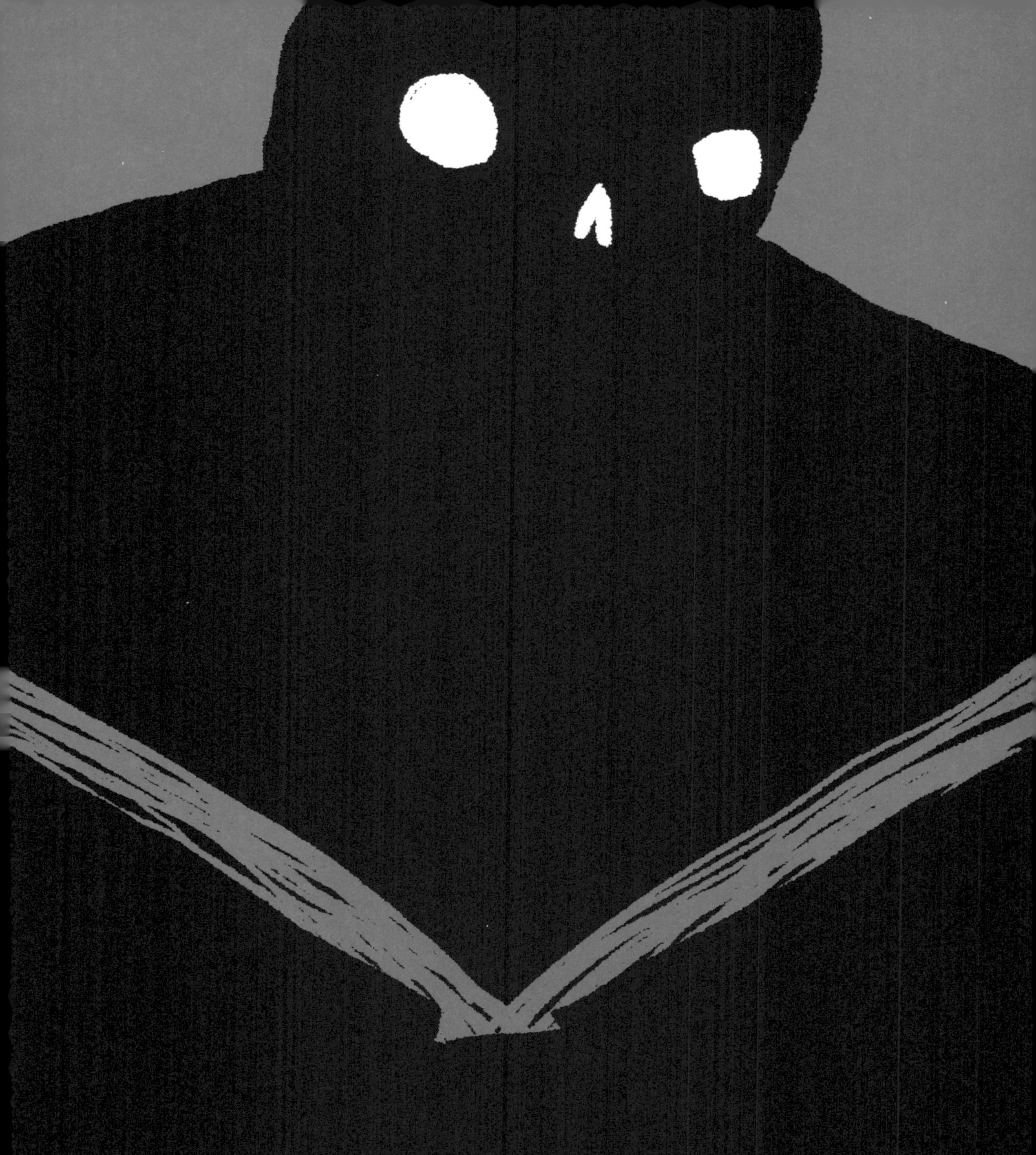

If my nightmare were true, my
father would have been able to start
telling his story about the skulls

The Book of Denial begins with skulls.

For a long time, it was believed that the skulls had been punctured after the infants' deaths. That those fractures were simply the result of the passage of centuries, as well as of natural elements and the chaotic looting of graves. Until more infant skulls were found with those same broken bones, in a cavern kept hermetically sealed since time immemorial.

It is the oldest proof that exists of the inhumanity of humankind: that for millions of years we have known how to bludgeon our own children to death.

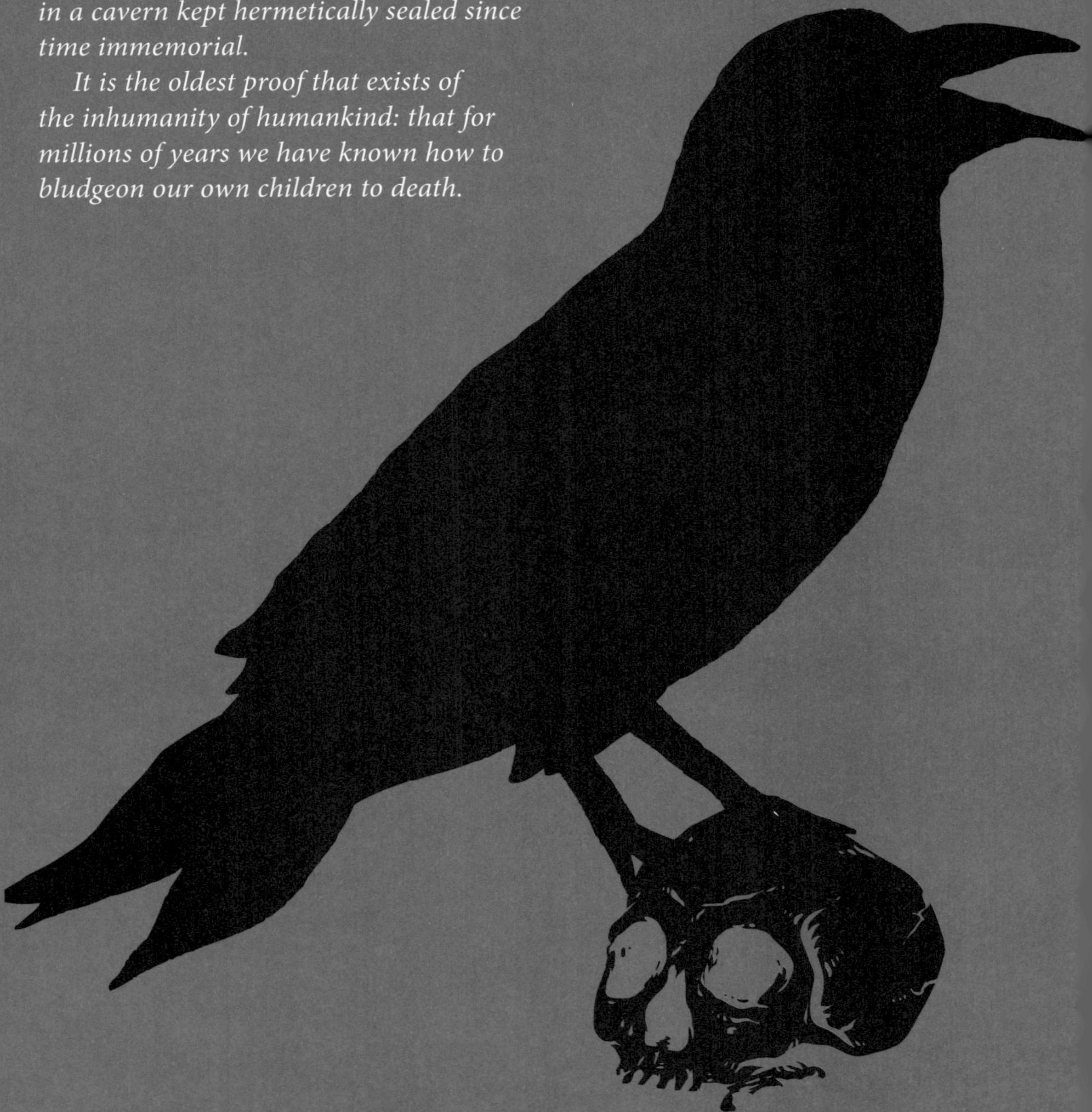

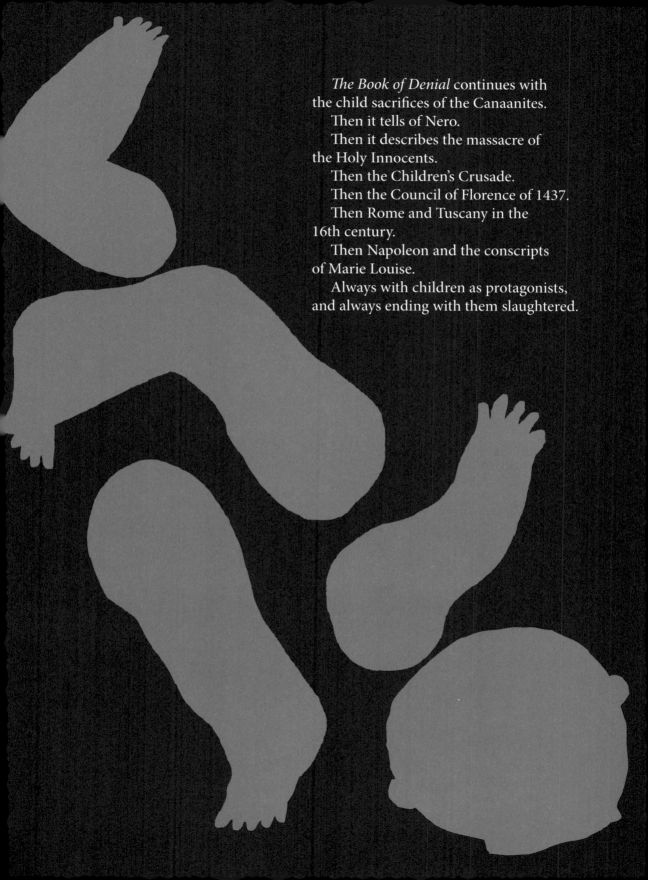

The Book of Denial continues with the child sacrifices of the Canaanites.
   Then it tells of Nero.
   Then it describes the massacre of the Holy Innocents.
   Then the Children's Crusade.
   Then the Council of Florence of 1437.
   Then Rome and Tuscany in the 16th century.
   Then Napoleon and the conscripts of Marie Louise.
   Always with children as protagonists, and always ending with them slaughtered.

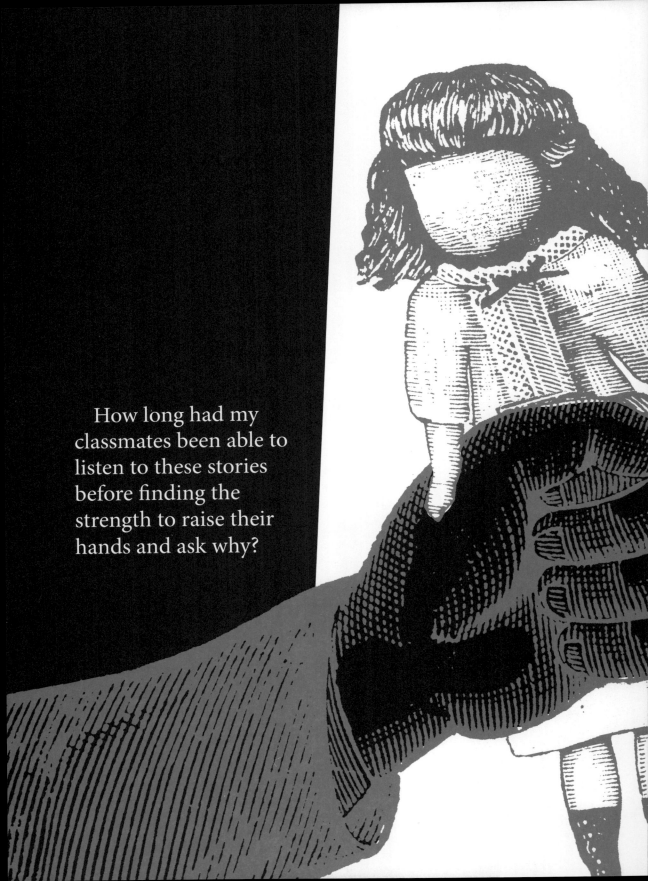

How long had my classmates been able to listen to these stories before finding the strength to raise their hands and ask why?

"Children must know this story of terror."

This was what Papá had said, that time he bent forward as if he were going to give Mamá a kiss.

But, instead of kissing her, he had whispered in her ear, "After all, this story belongs to them."

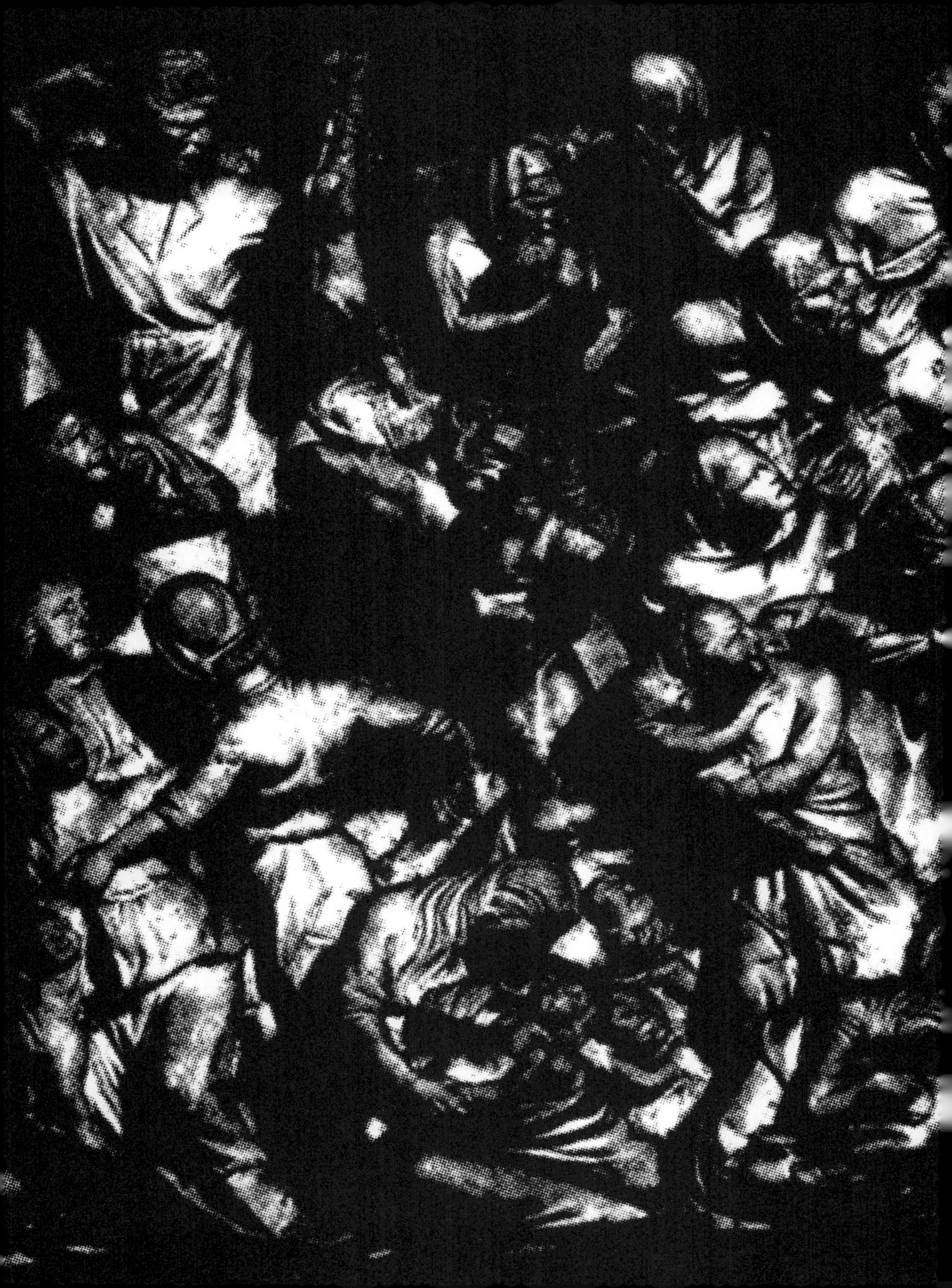

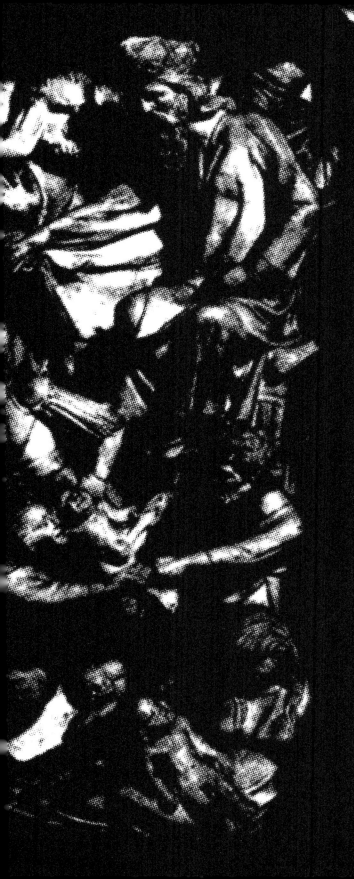

I've always liked horror stories because I thought they honored an agreement, the same way that all the games of the world follow rules.

The rule of games: This is not real. No game is real.

And the rule for horror stories? They are not true. No story should be true.

Papá keeps wandering through the house. From bedroom to bedroom, from the living room back to the dining room, from downstairs to upstairs.

His hair is uncombed, his eyes are red, his face is now as pale as salt.

Sometimes he manages to reach the door of his study, and even grabs the door handle. He stays like that for a long time—still, unable to open the door, but unable to walk away.

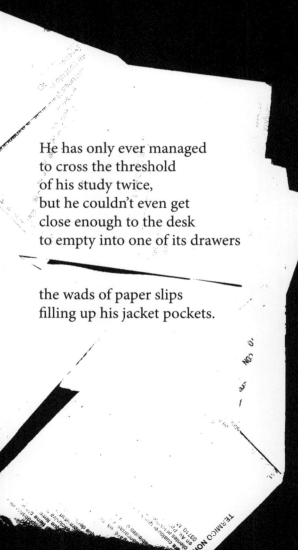

He has only ever managed
to cross the threshold
of his study twice,
but he couldn't even get
close enough to the desk
to empty into one of its drawers

the wads of paper slips
filling up his jacket pockets.

He hasn't opened *The Book of Denial* for days. He didn't even look at it when he went into the study those two times.

But this afternoon, I open the notebook when I slip into the study, when Mamá and Papá are nowhere to be found.

Where before there were pages as still and waveless as a calm sea, there is now another story.

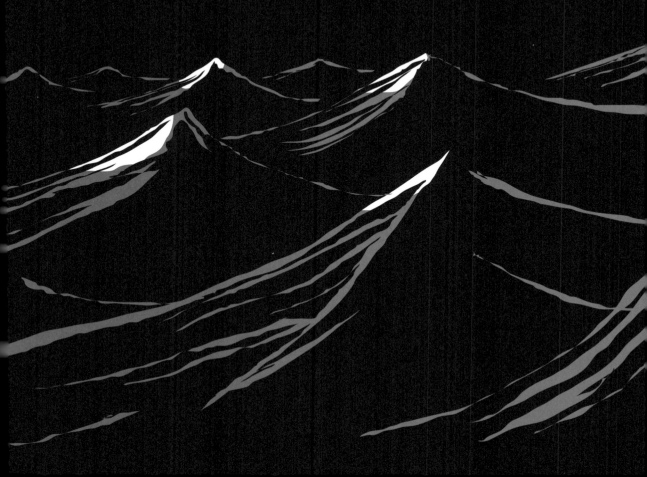

A storm.
That's what words
are sometimes.
A storm.

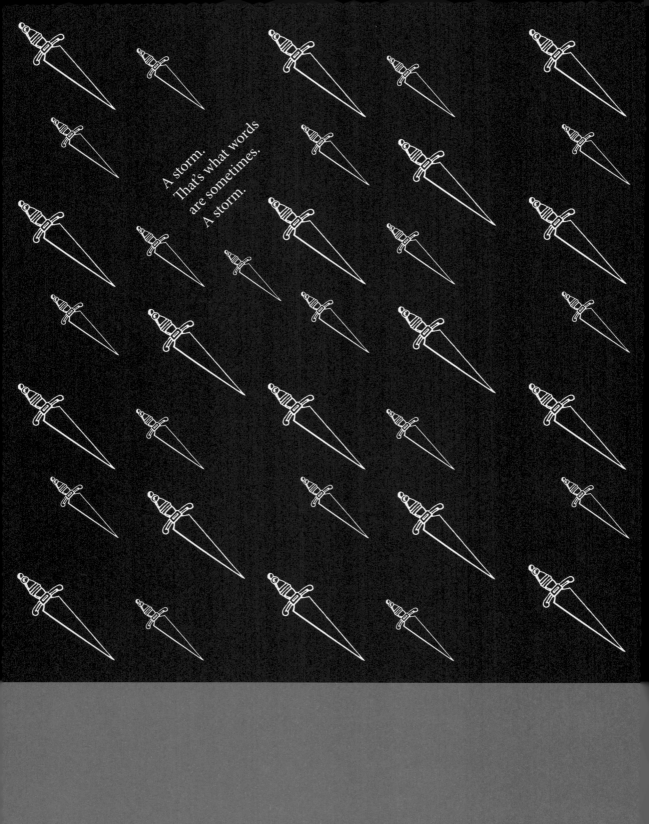

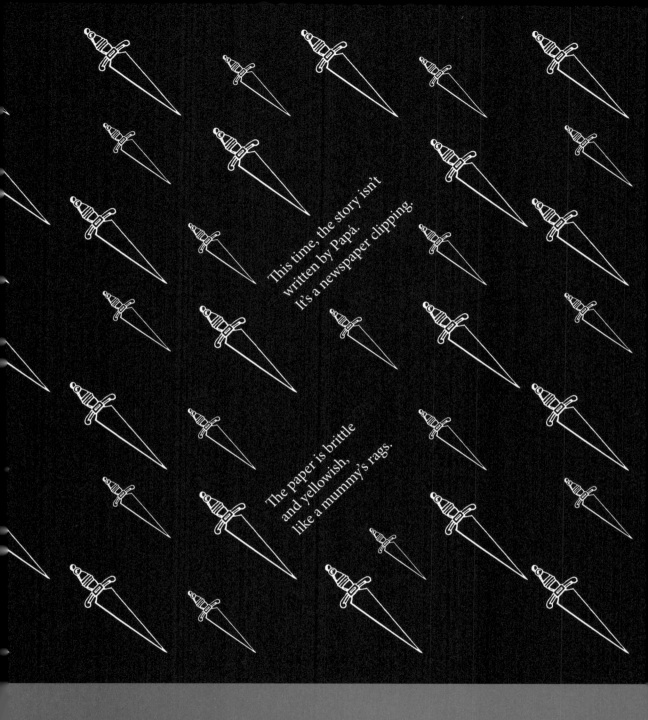

This time, the story isn't written by Papá. It's a newspaper clipping.

The paper is brittle and yellowish, like a mummy's rags.

It says that over four years, 3,900 babies disappeared.

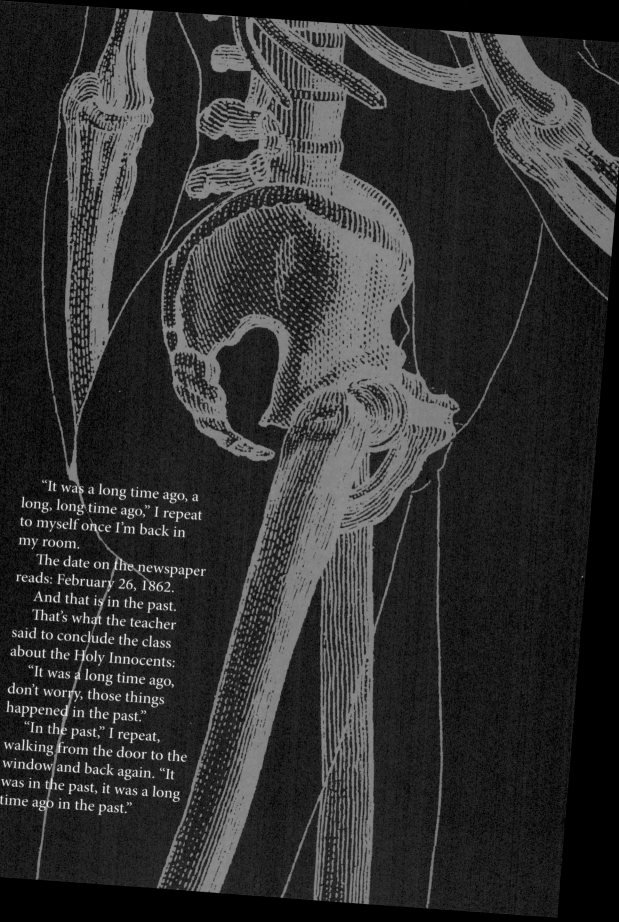

"It was a long time ago, a long, long time ago," I repeat to myself once I'm back in my room.

The date on the newspaper reads: February 26, 1862.

And that is in the past. That's what the teacher said to conclude the class about the Holy Innocents:

"It was a long time ago, don't worry, those things happened in the past."

"In the past," I repeat, walking from the door to the window and back again. "It was in the past, it was a long time ago in the past."

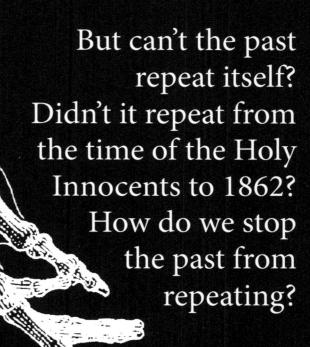

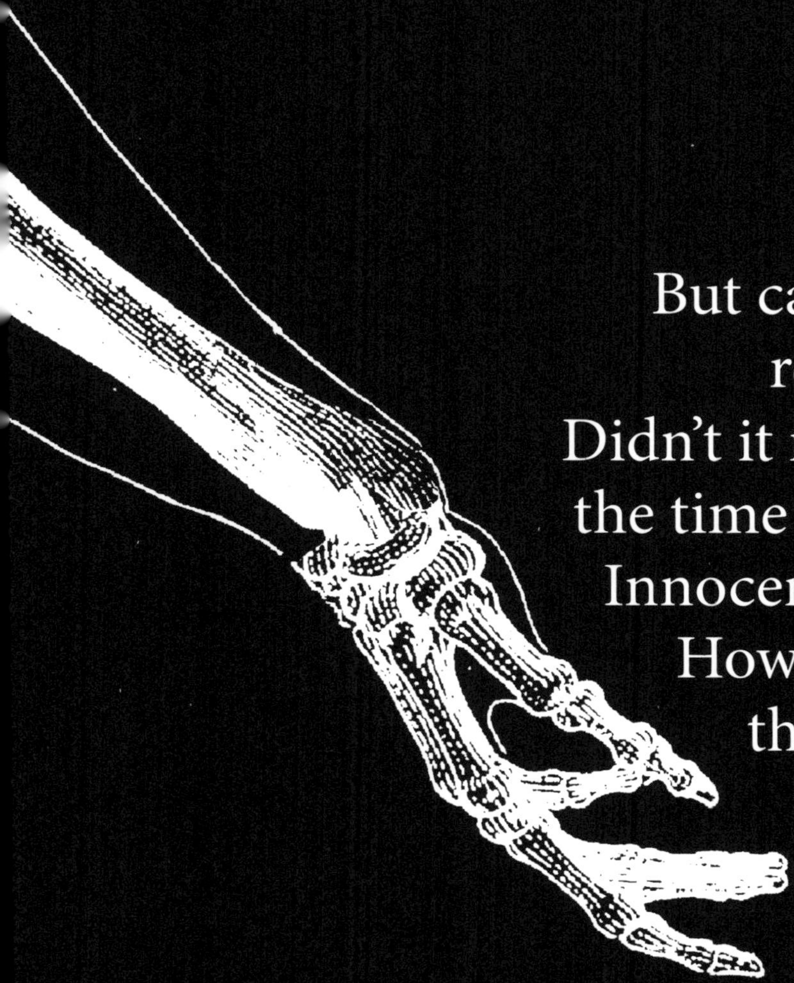

But can't the past repeat itself? Didn't it repeat from the time of the Holy Innocents to 1862? How do we stop the past from repeating?

How do we stop time from moving forward?

What is moving forward,
without Papá's help, is his book.

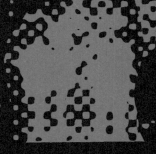

This morning, before going to school, I found another newspaper clipping, dated November 15, 1900. It was about families who adopted children and asked for money to feed them. They were farmers who lived far from the cities, who brought the adopted children to their farms and locked them in their cellars. Then those women and men stuffed their ears with scraps of cloth, so as not to hear the wails of the children as they died of hunger.

The teacher is writing the date on the blackboard: October 20, 2010.

I look at all my classmates, but they seem calm.

Only 110 years separate us from the events in Papá's book. And my classmates are all so calm.

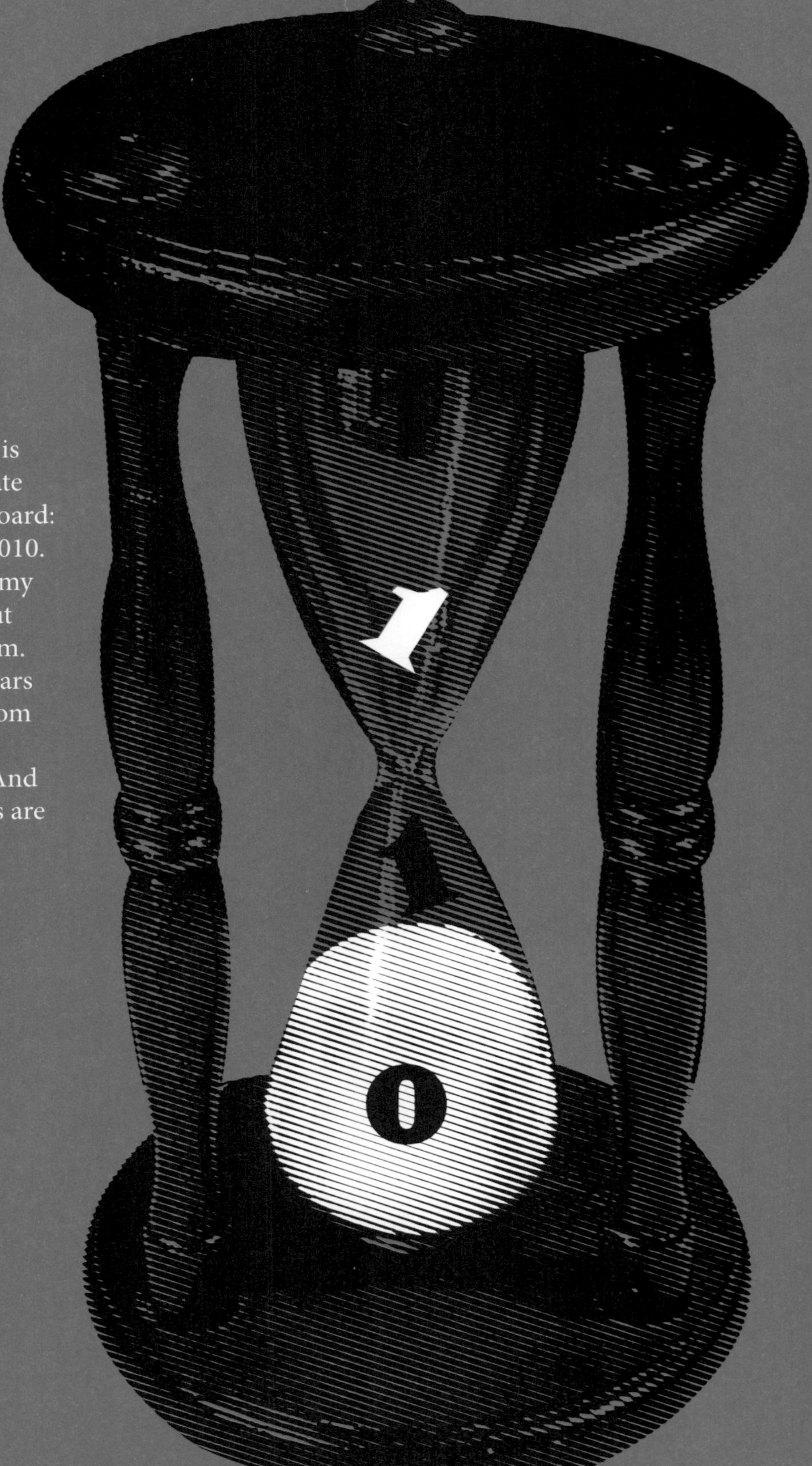
1
0

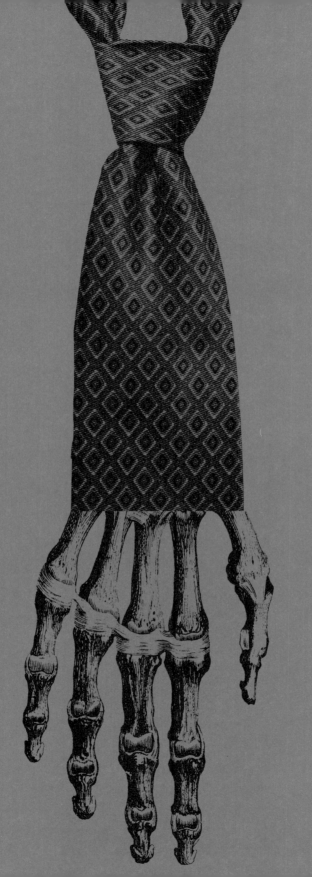

My Papá. He is my father. He is my father, but these are not his stories.
I think now that I would prefer it if they were his own, if he had invented them, if these horror stories only ever happened inside his book.

Because horror stories are so suspenseful, I usually read them fast. I even skip entire pages to reach each horrible moment as quickly as possible.

But the best horror stories are those I'm barely able to read for even a few lines. I start to read, but suddenly shut the book.

I slam it shut without thinking, as if I've seen a spider.

And then I break out in chills, certain that the spider is still there inside the book, waiting for me, for whenever I dare to open it again.

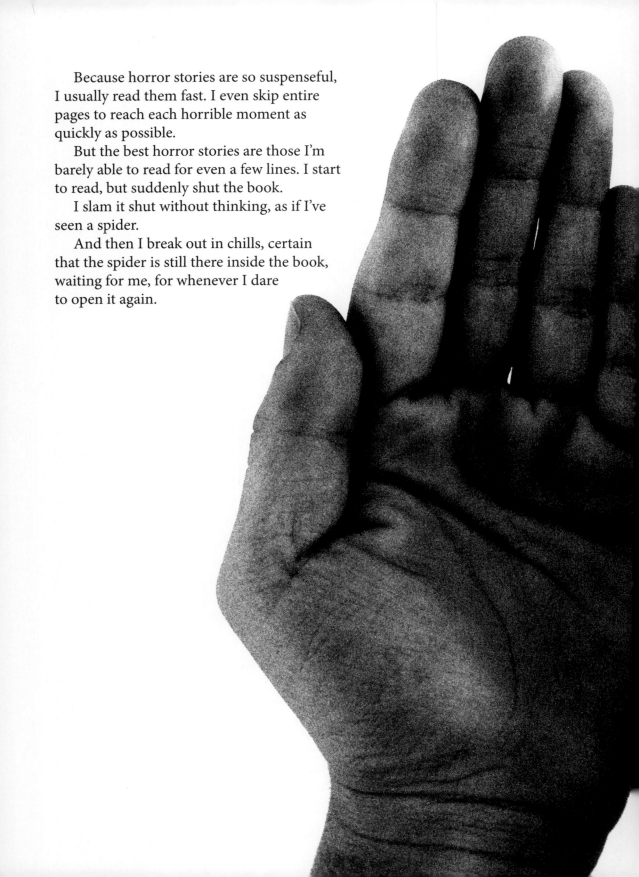

What would it feel like to suddenly discover spiders coming out of your hands?

I wonder because of Papá. He's always holding his hands in front of his eyes and staring at them as if he can't recognize them.

As if he's waiting for the moment when his hands fill with eggs that will hatch into spiders that crawl between his fingers.

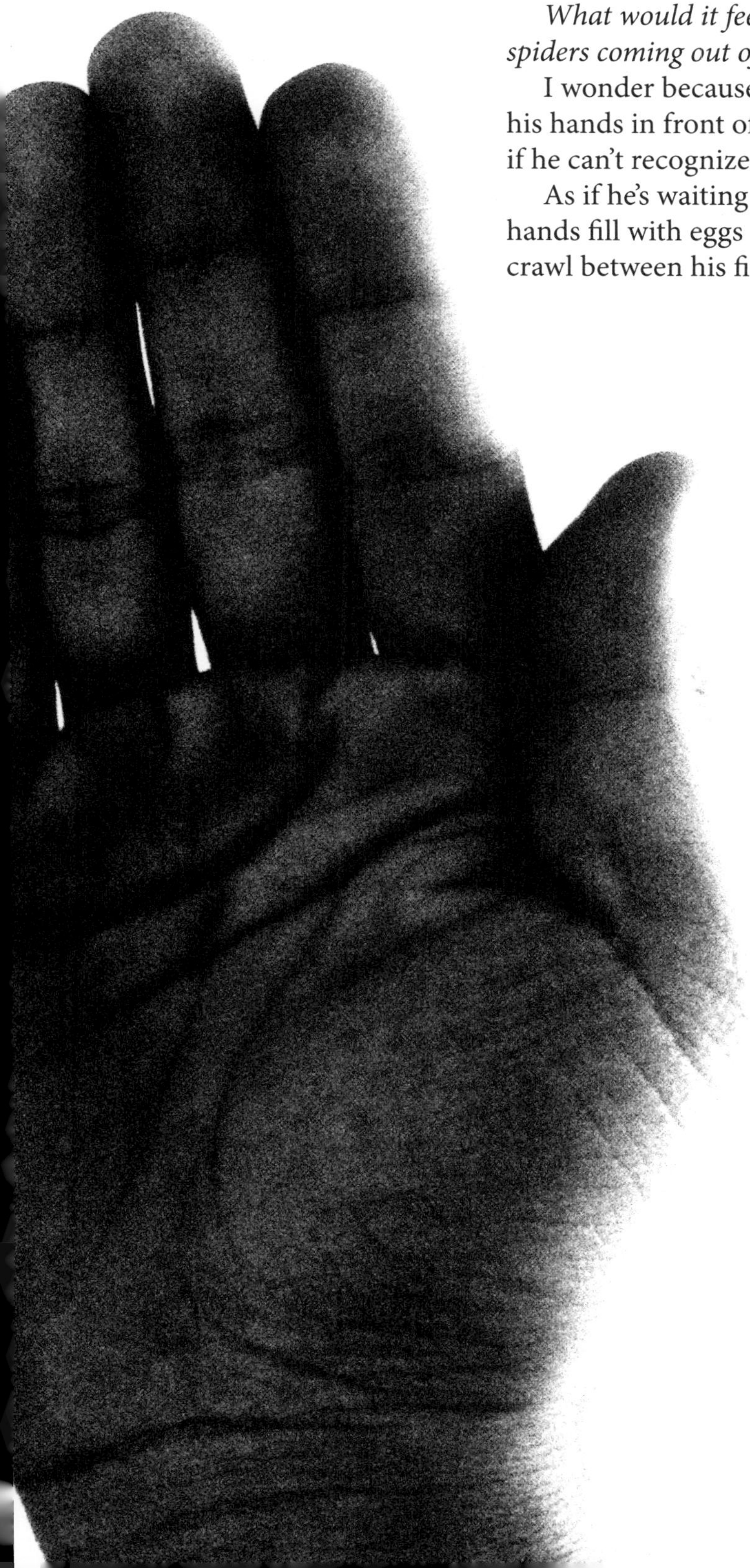

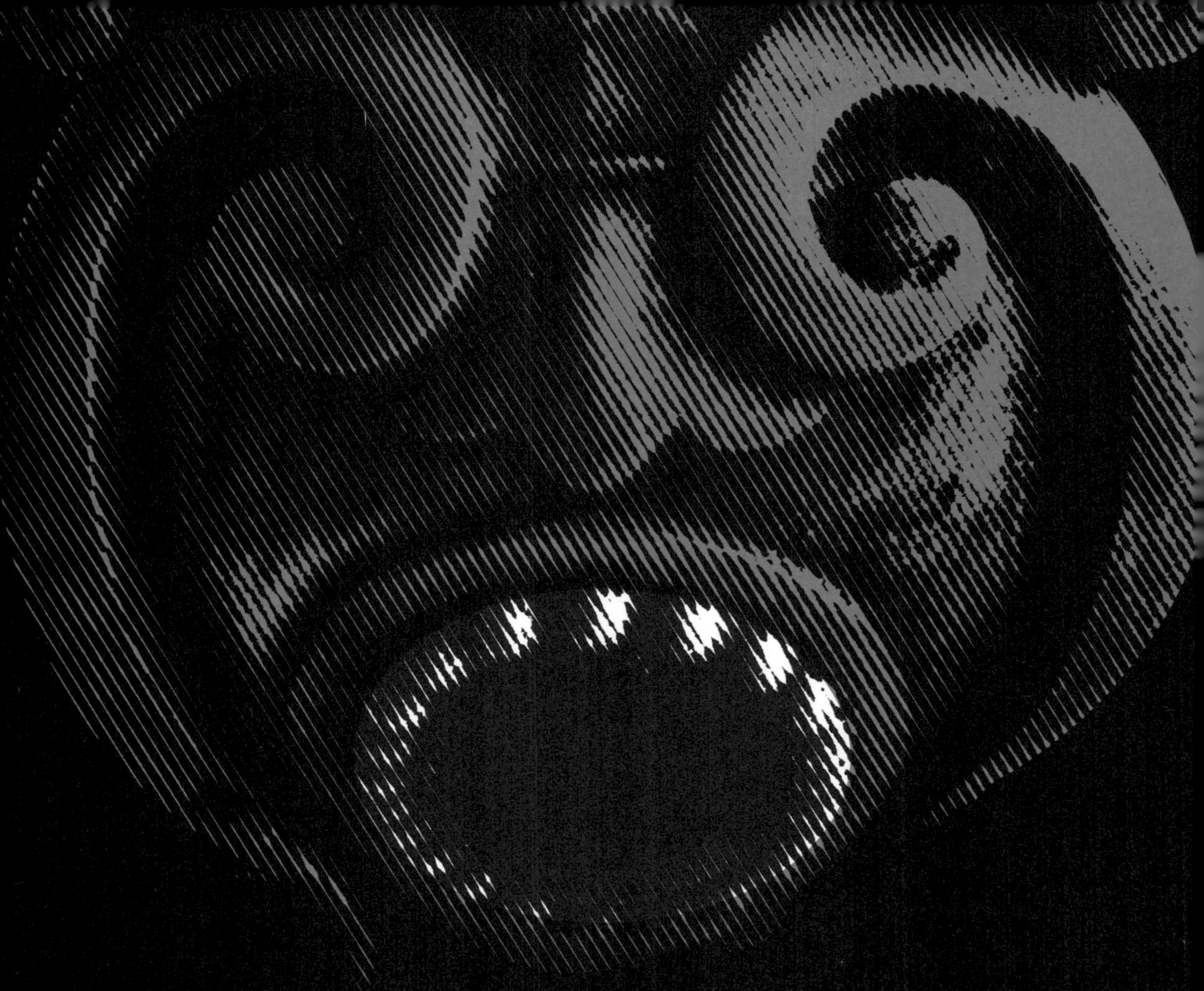

Papá grows increasingly more gaunt,
more haggard, more restless.
I think he wants to stop writing,
but he doesn't seem to have a choice.
So today, I've decided that
I'm going to help him.
Not like Mamá did, when she brought me
my books and backpack and told me
about the long path to obligation.
I am going to do exactly the opposite.

On my way to school, I take
a detour toward the park. I pass
various trash cans, a small lake,
and other promising spots.
The well seems
like the best place to me.
It's sealed with a thick wooden
cover held in place by locks and
chains, but there's just enough space

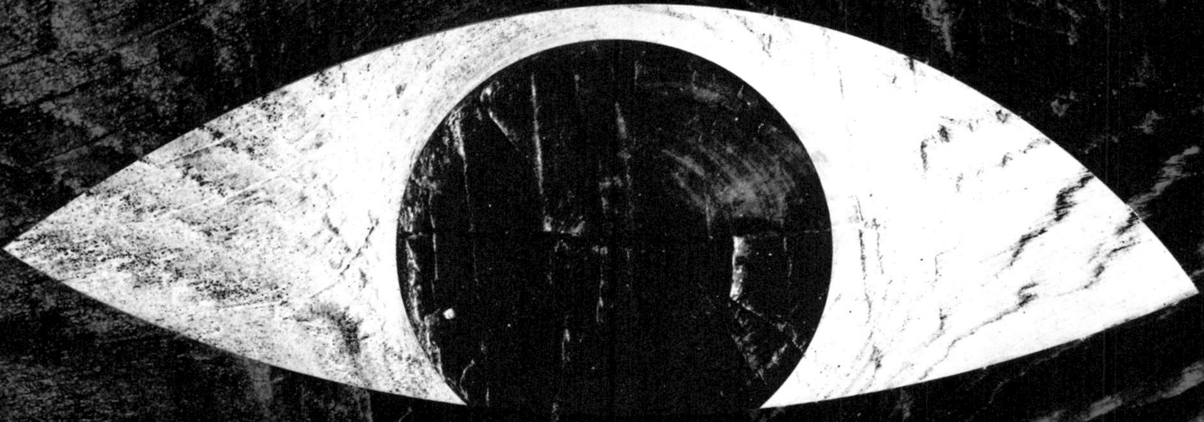

between the edge of the well
and the wooden cover
for Papá's book to fit.
I'm able to slide it into that gap,
but have to push really hard for it
to disappear inside.
Although I put my ear to the slit
right away, I don't hear anything
but silence.

Papá still hasn't realized that *The Book of Denial* doesn't exist anymore.

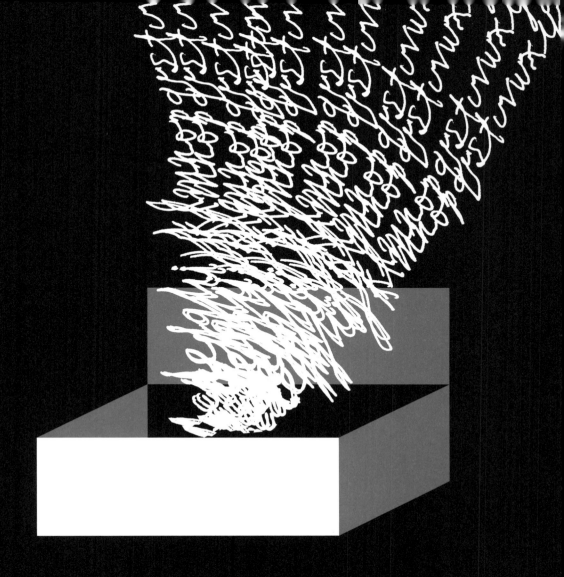

   I've never seen Mamá tear up the letter she keeps in her drawer, but I know she must have done so.
   The piece of paper, which she unfolds from time to time to read until she cries, is sometimes white like the original letter. But at other times, the paper is pale green or blue or yellowish.
   I suppose Mamá knows the words of the letter by heart. So, she only has to write them down again on each new sheet she puts away in the drawer.

What I can't imagine is Papá knowing so many words by heart...

When I woke up this morning, a hardcover notebook—which was not the hardcover notebook that I pushed down the well—was on top of his desk.

Inside were all those same words, tilted as if by the wind and undulating like waves, telling the most terrible story in the world once more.

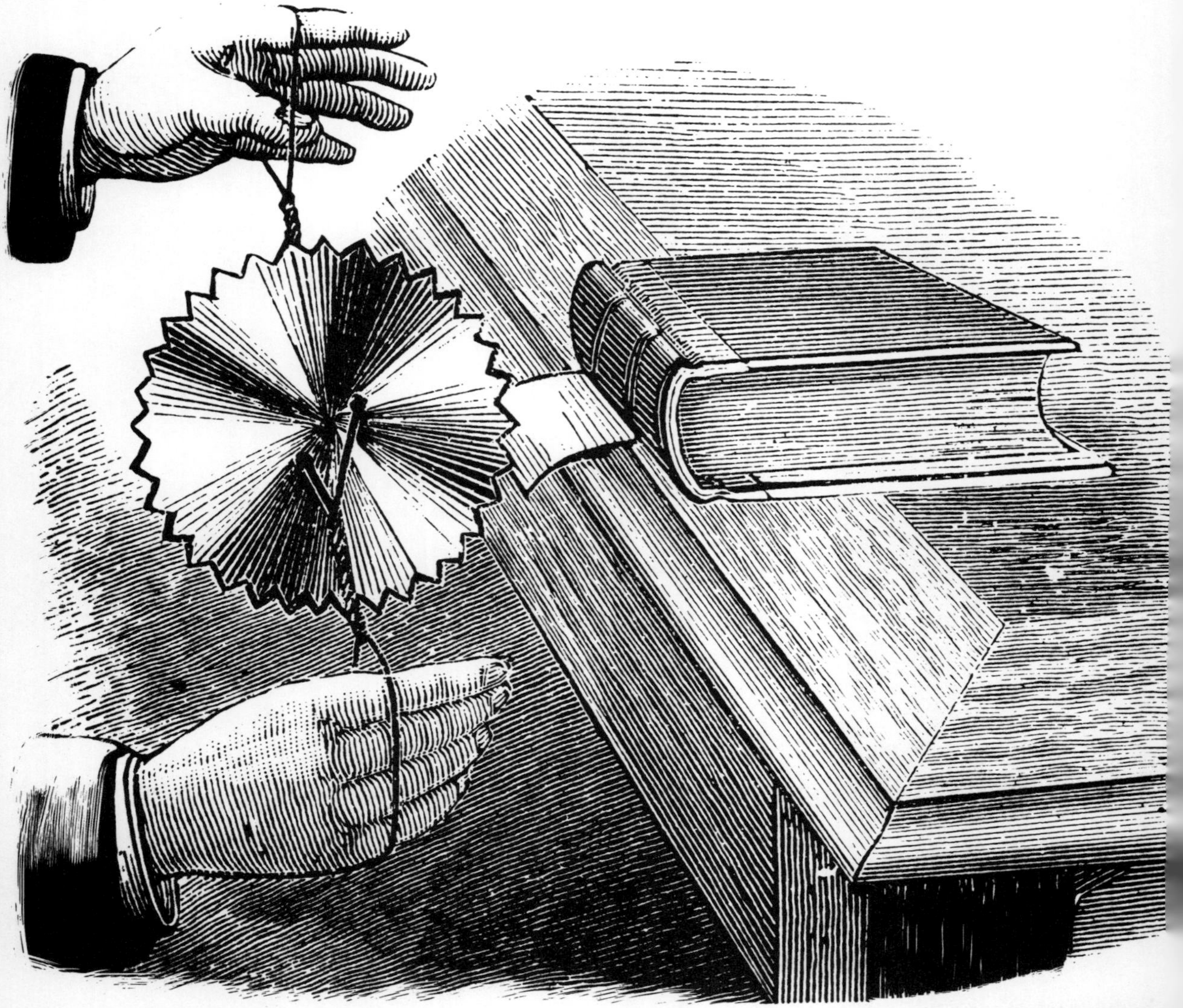

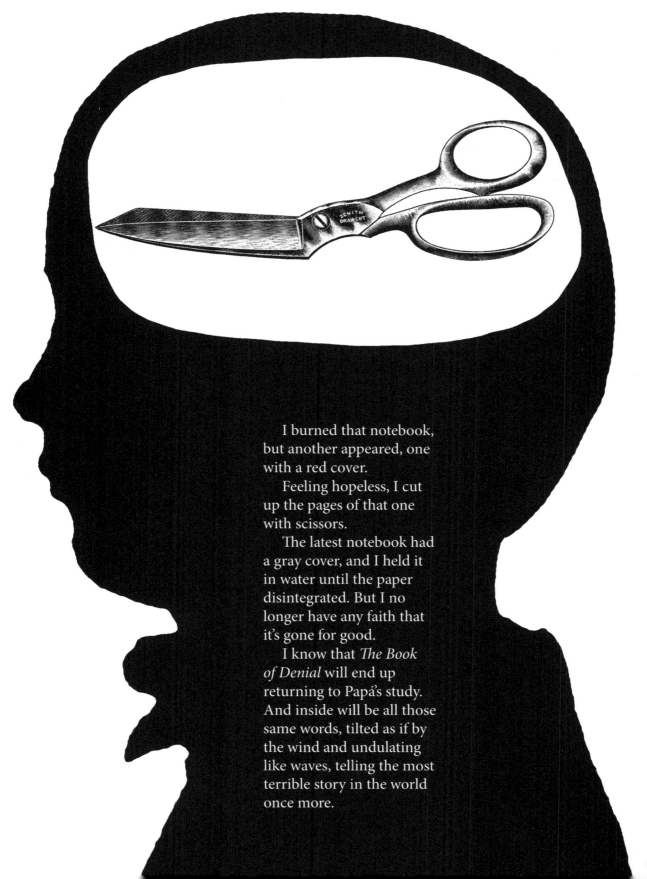

I burned that notebook, but another appeared, one with a red cover.

Feeling hopeless, I cut up the pages of that one with scissors.

The latest notebook had a gray cover, and I held it in water until the paper disintegrated. But I no longer have any faith that it's gone for good.

I know that *The Book of Denial* will end up returning to Papá's study. And inside will be all those same words, tilted as if by the wind and undulating like waves, telling the most terrible story in the world once more.

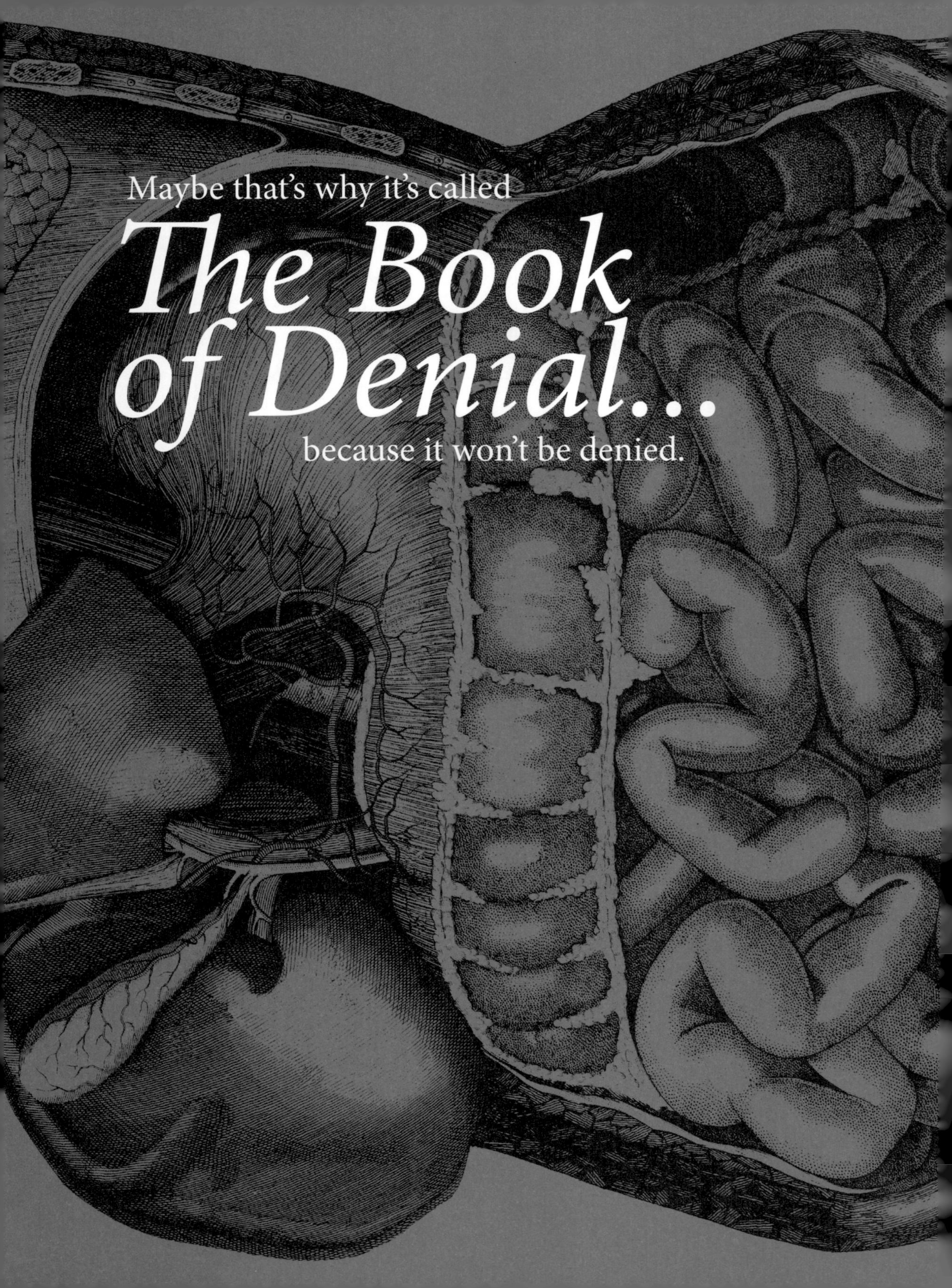
Maybe that's why it's called
The Book
of Denial...
because it won't be denied.

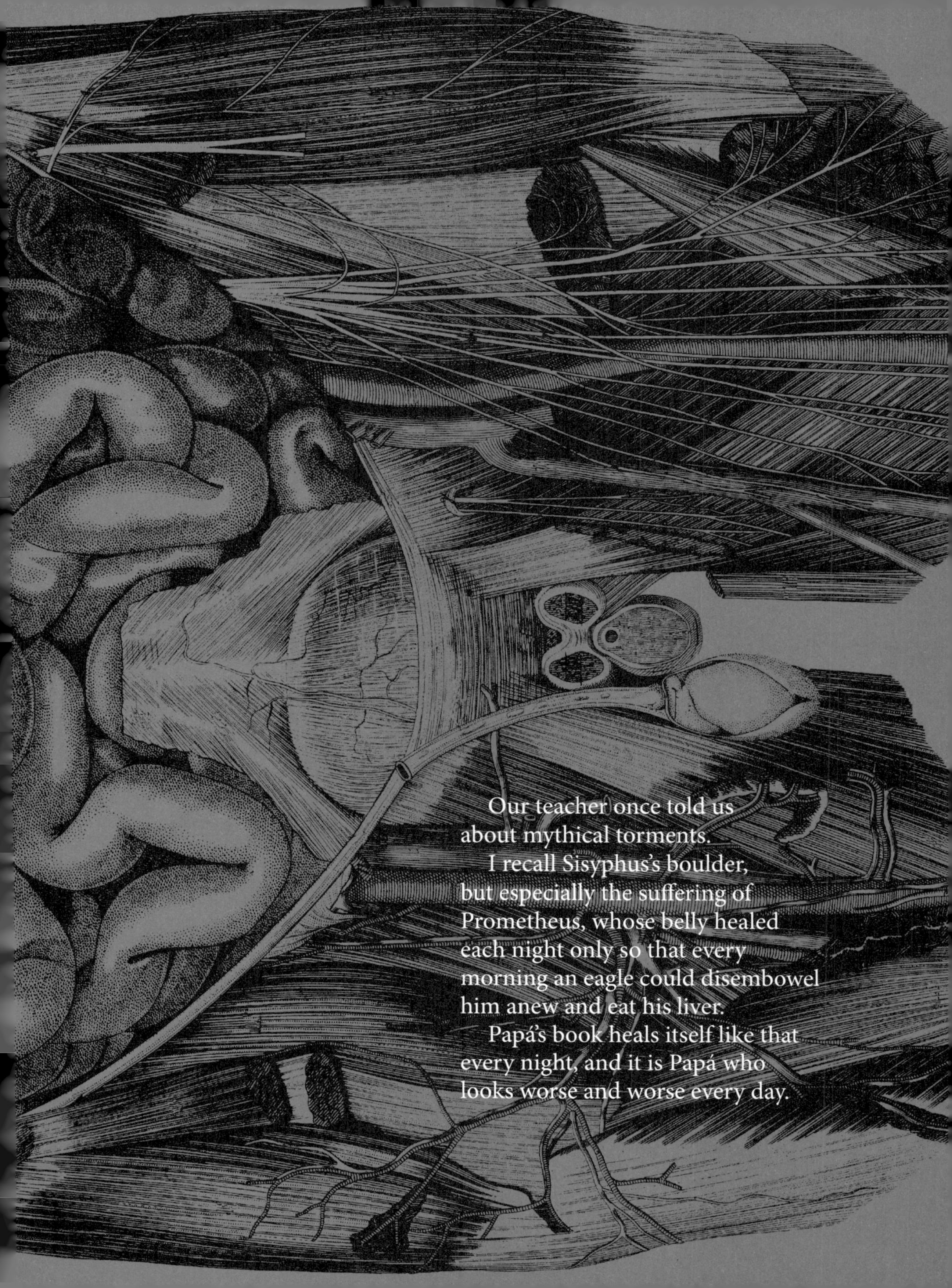

Our teacher once told us about mythical torments.

I recall Sisyphus's boulder, but especially the suffering of Prometheus, whose belly healed each night only so that every morning an eagle could disembowel him anew and eat his liver.

Papá's book heals itself like that every night, and it is Papá who looks worse and worse every day.

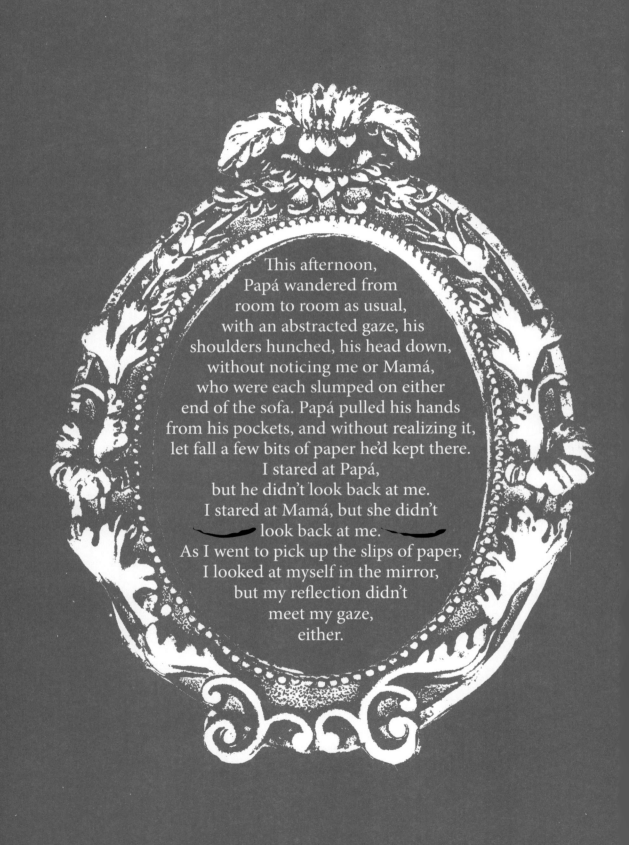

This afternoon,
Papá wandered from
room to room as usual,
with an abstracted gaze, his
shoulders hunched, his head down,
without noticing me or Mamá,
who were each slumped on either
end of the sofa. Papá pulled his hands
from his pockets, and without realizing it,
let fall a few bits of paper he'd kept there.
I stared at Papá,
but he didn't look back at me.
I stared at Mamá, but she didn't
look back at me.
As I went to pick up the slips of paper,
I looked at myself in the mirror,
but my reflection didn't
meet my gaze,
either.

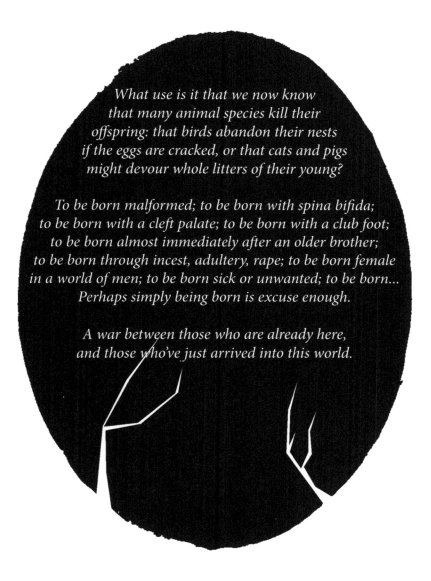

What use is it that we now know that many animal species kill their offspring: that birds abandon their nests if the eggs are cracked, or that cats and pigs might devour whole litters of their young?

To be born malformed; to be born with spina bifida; to be born with a cleft palate; to be born with a club foot; to be born almost immediately after an older brother; to be born through incest, adultery, rape; to be born female in a world of men; to be born sick or unwanted; to be born... Perhaps simply being born is excuse enough.

A war between those who are already here, and those who've just arrived into this world.

That is what I read in those pages.

For almost the entire history of the world, the killing of children has been a murder that no one investigates, for which no one demands justice, in which there are no accusers because there are no afflicted parties; a murder that is kept secret, to which all are indifferent, which we tacitly agree to ignore.

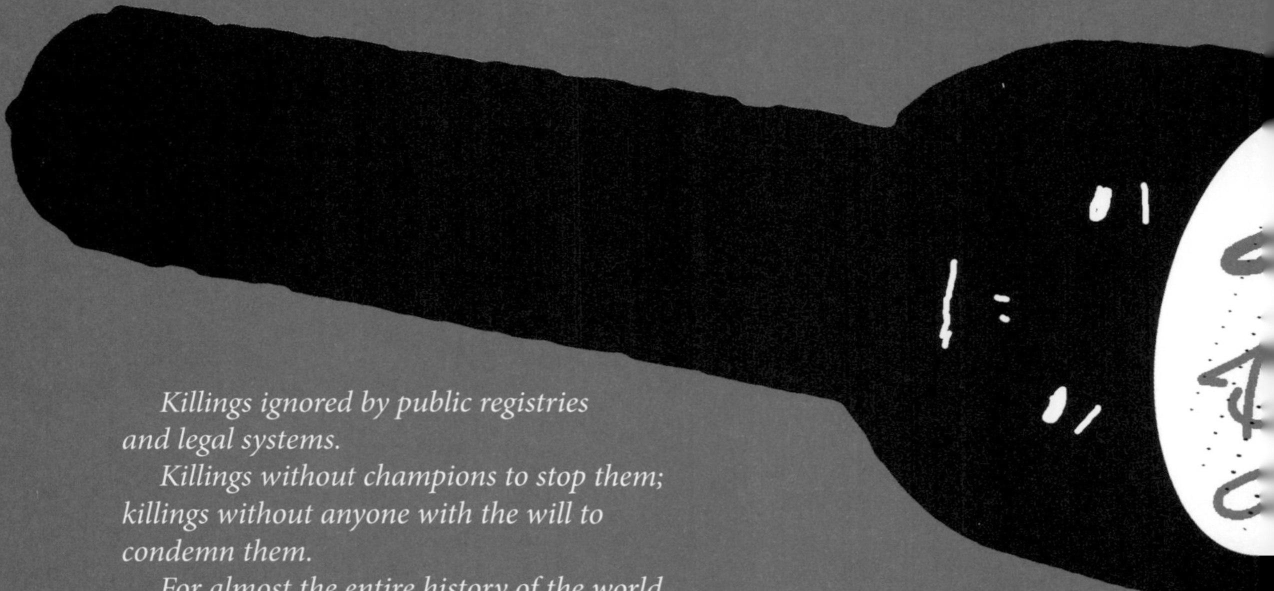

Killings ignored by public registries and legal systems.

Killings without champions to stop them; killings without anyone with the will to condemn them.

For almost the entire history of the world...

Today, our era seems different, but this is mere appearance. Still, perhaps that is enough to permit us to speak of this now.

We cannot allow children to continue to disappear in our time without putting that disappearance into words.

I must write this so that others will care... and so that I will continue to care... So long as it still matters to me... So long as it still matters to us... So long as it seems to matter to us... So long as it seems that words have some purpose...

Yes, this is Papa's writing, undulating like waves, that I read under the blankets by flashlight.

Yes, this is why the book has kept advancing.

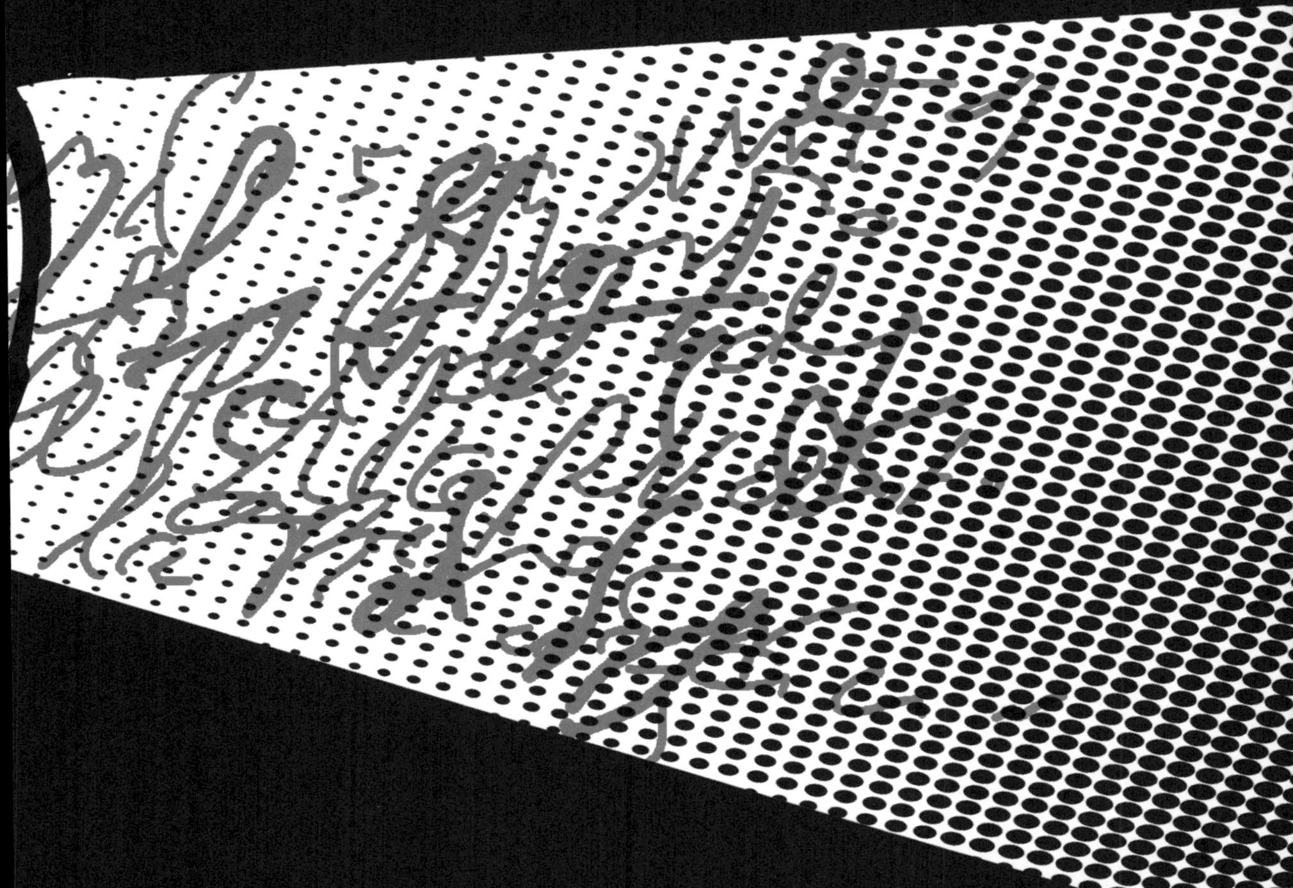

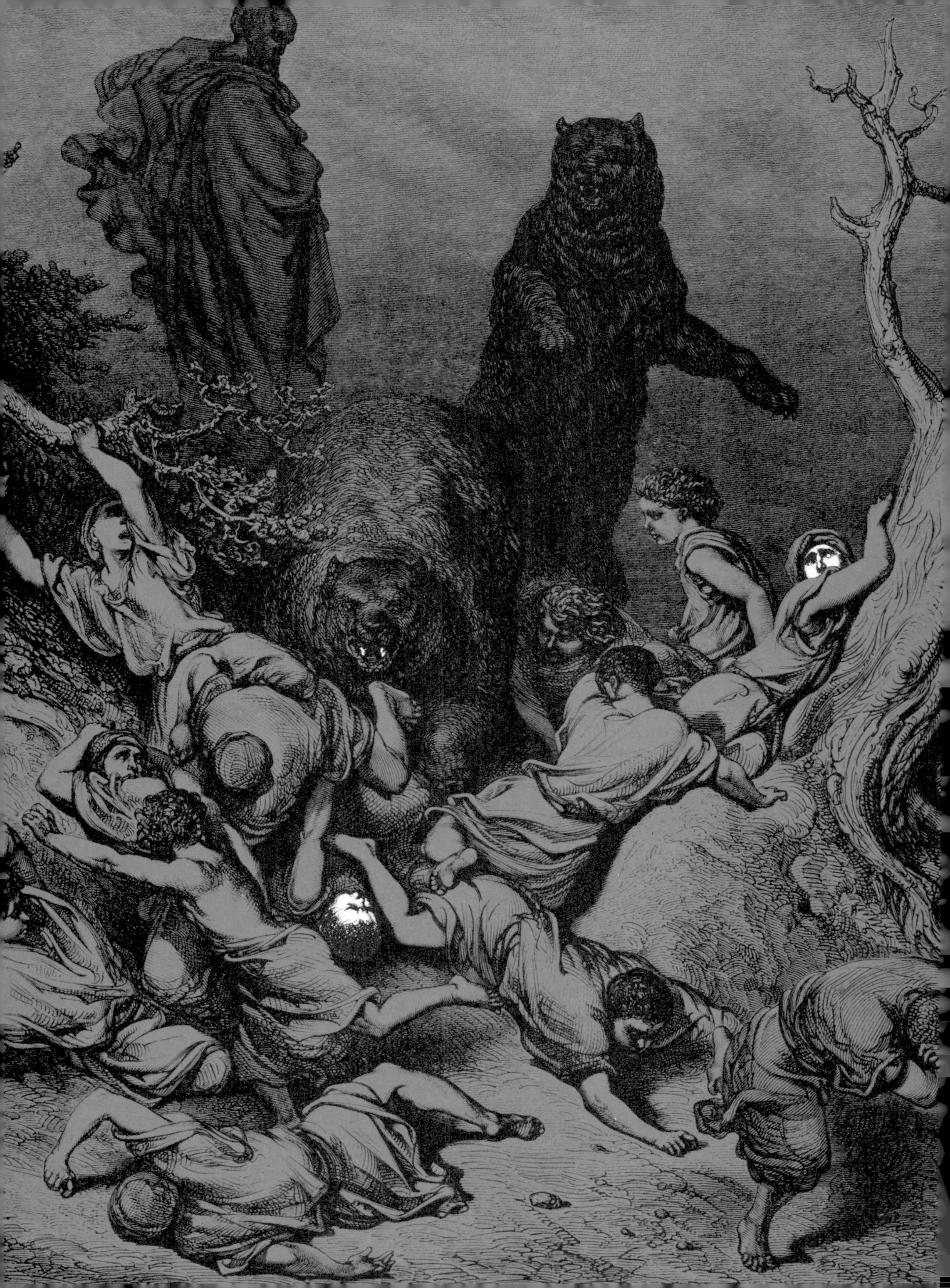

by anyone who is a cynic.
We are used to seeing the terror of children. We know
they suffer nightmares in which they are devoured
or chopped into pieces,
and we think that's just how life is.
We have grown used to seeing them awaken
screaming in panic because in their dreams,
they are being chased by threatening figures.
We think this is part of childhood,
a normal component of mental life...
But it is not normal, that is not just how life is;
we must not become accustomed
to children suffering like this.
To begin, let us consider their size:
Is there anyone more killable than a child?
The worst thing of all is that all of us were once children,
and we have all forgotten that.
The worst thing of all is that we have forgotten
that as children, we had fears
and were terrified by those fears.
That fear we all had: They're going to kill me.
It is what we've forgotten: We once knew
what all children know.

DID I, TOO, ONCE HAVE THAT FEAR? DID I, TOO, FORGET IT?

I read each scrap of paper on which Papá had written until I reached the very last one.

It was the only one I couldn't chew or swallow, as I'd done with all the rest.

I put it under my pillow, very close to my head, and all night I listened to it whisper in my ear:

Why haven't we been able to change this story of terror?

To change this story of terror.

The teacher has written the date on the blackboard: October 27. Class today begins with history, where it seems that we children have never existed.

How can something change if its very existence is denied from the outset?

Now I think that's why Papá's book is called ***The Book of Denial.***

What about the children of Greece?

The children of Rome?

The children of India?

The children of the Middle Ages?

I feel like raising my hand and asking my teacher,
"Why does history never talk about us?"
But I don't, because my hand is busy doing something more important.
Then I speak without asking permission.

"Where was history when the children were murdered?"

At first I ask it in a murmur, but then
I start to shout it with more and more force.

"Where was history?"

But no one pays any attention to me.

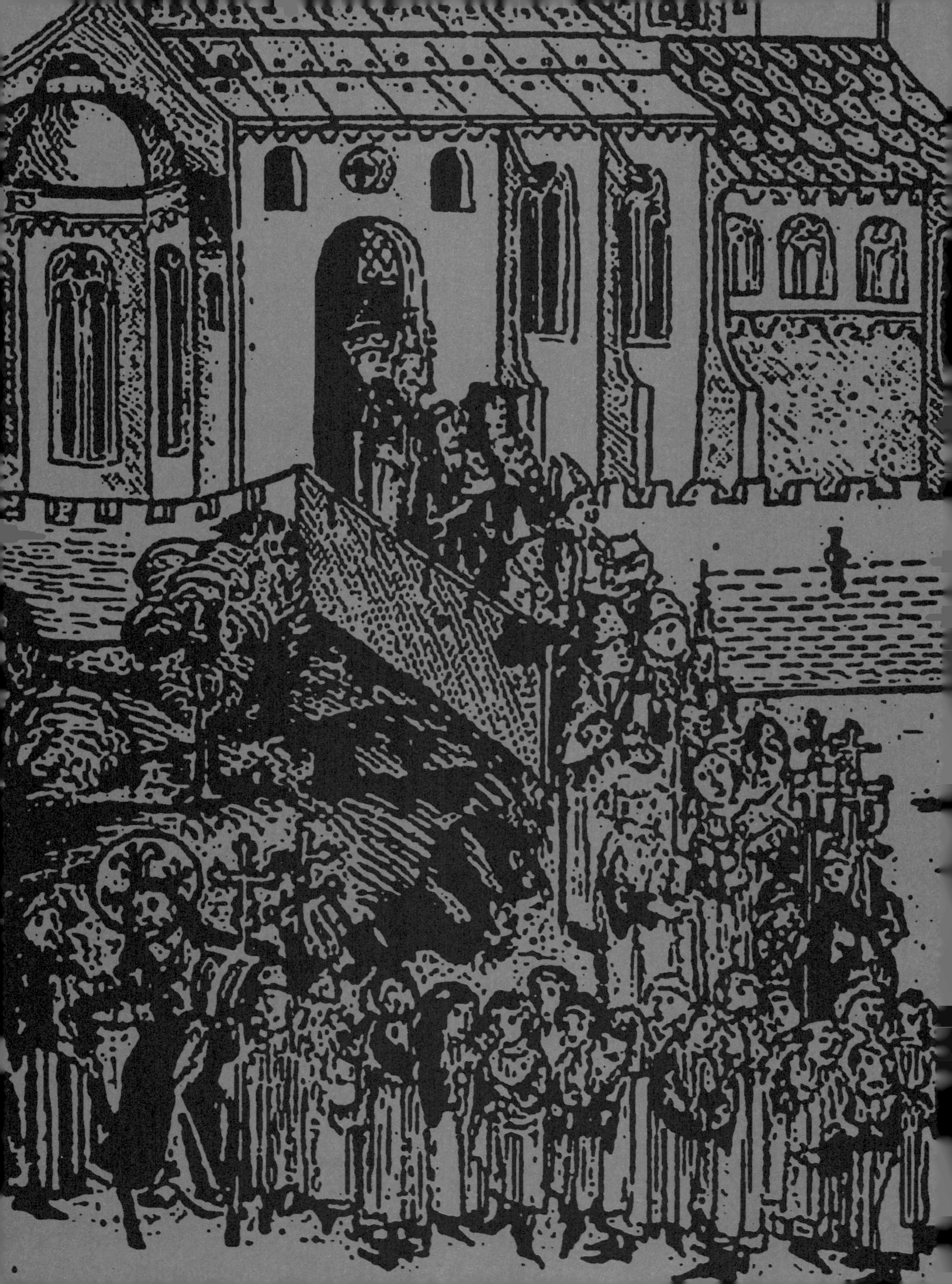

“In the Middle Ages, hundreds of thousands of children crossed Europe to reach the seacoasts. It was said that God would open the waters so that His army of children could reach Jerusalem and reconquer it.

“The sea never opened.”

As I sharpen my pencil, I hear myself repeating these words, which means that I must know *The Book of Denial* by heart, too.

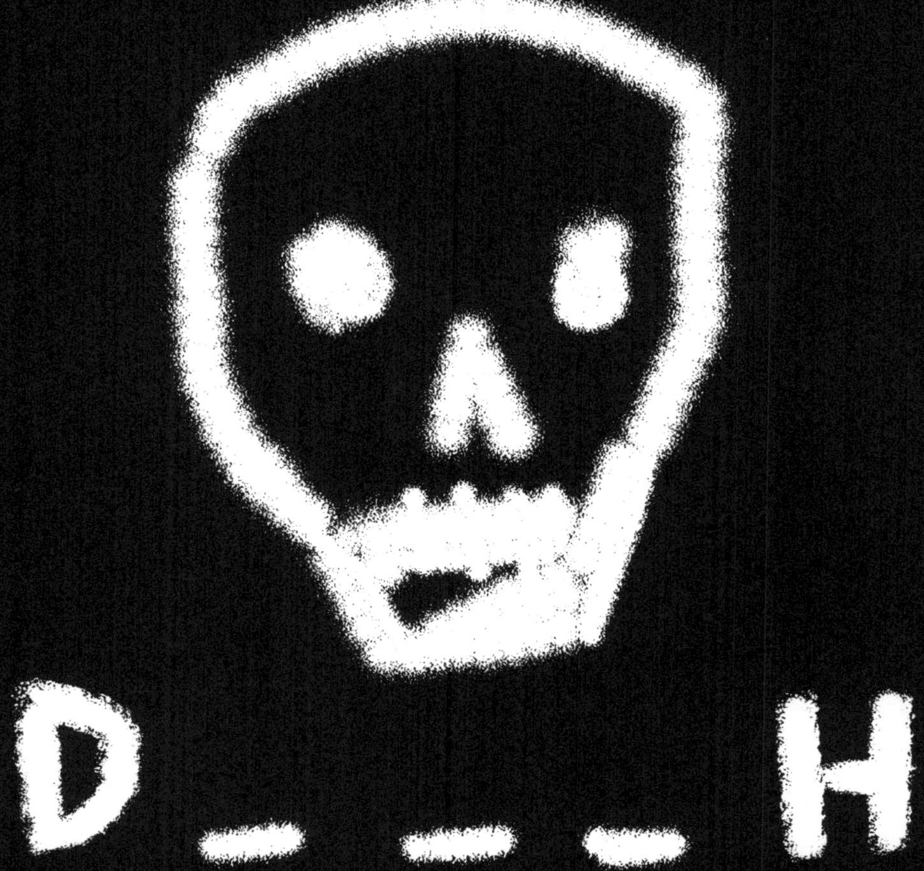
D _ _ _ H

As always, my teacher doesn’t pay any attention to me.

As always, each of my classmates ignores me.

Not even María turns to glance over her shoulder, as she used to, to look towards the back of the room where I sit.

Everything is just like it always is, but I know it’s not the same.

This time they know, they intuit in some way, or they must have found out, that I am doing something very important, which is why they don’t wish to disturb me.

The teacher has erased the 7 from the date this morning, and in its place has drawn an 8: October 28.

I keep writing.

Yesterday, I erased my marks just like the teacher does with the numbers of the date. I erased all the letters that emerged from my hand, badly tilted and badly undulating in my notebook, until I got tired, and today I've started to cross them out.

I am imitating the writing
on the little unfolded bits of
paper I have on top of my desk,
because I want to learn
to write like Papá.

I will never be a writer.
I will never have books published.
I will never have a shelf full of my ideas.
I have only one idea.

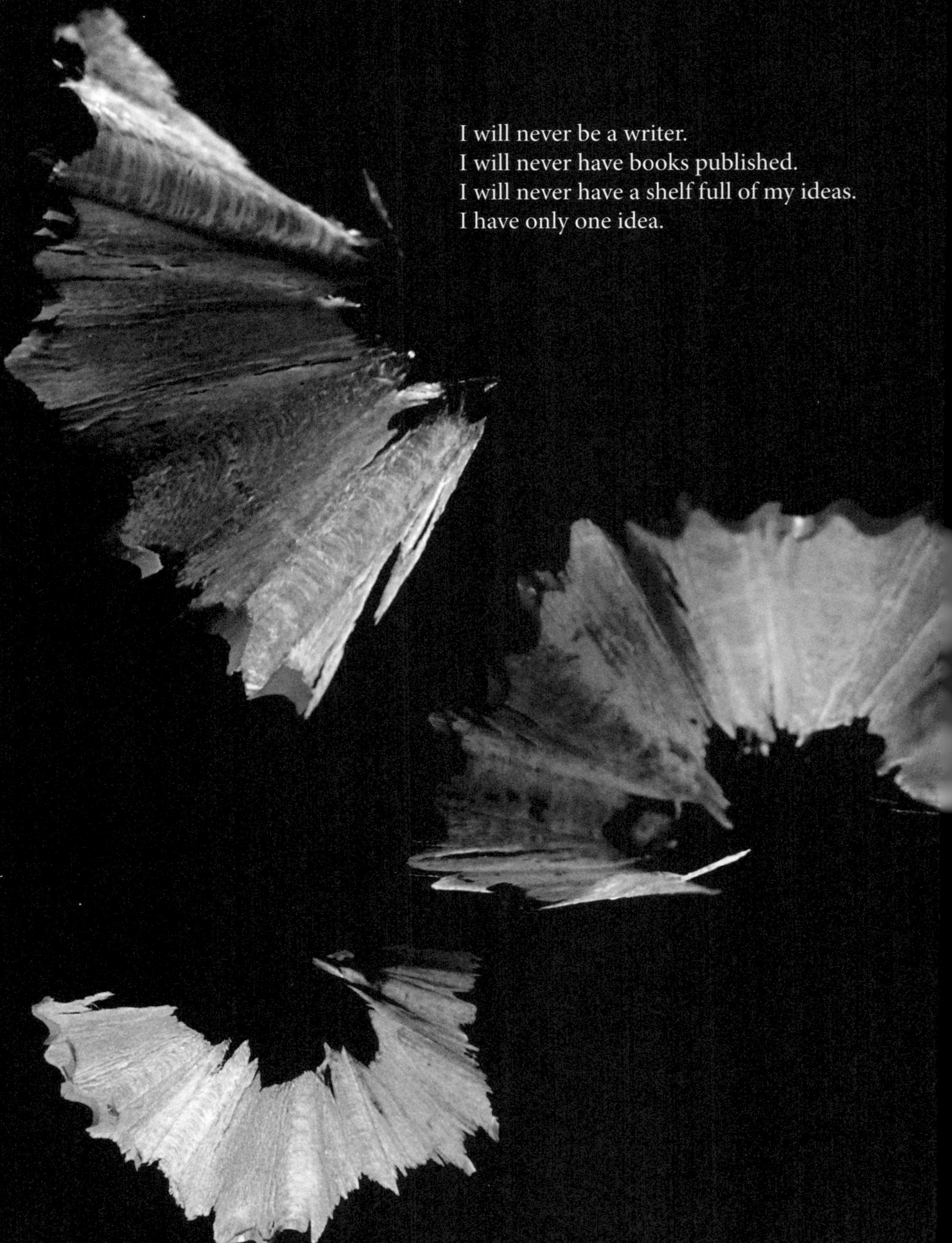

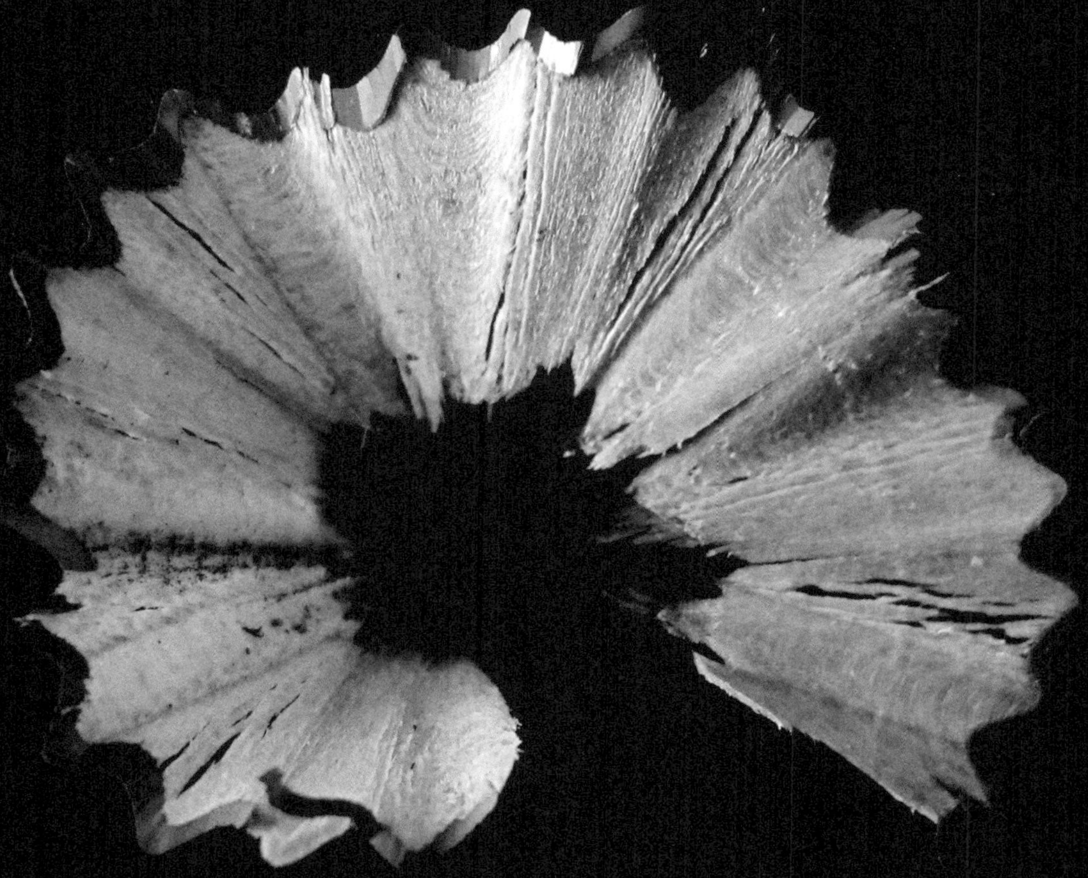

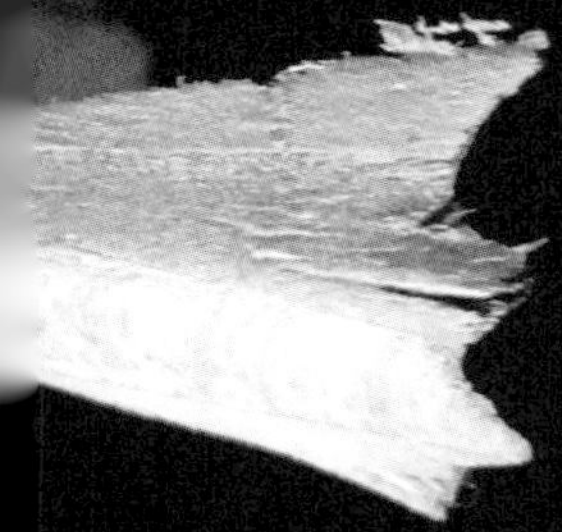

I sharpen my pencil, and I write.
And so I advance through my notebook.
And so the morning advances.
And so I advance toward the tilted letters
of *The Book of Denial.*

October 29.
Still the same, single idea.

Even though my eyes ache and my hand hurts, what helps me keep writing is the thought that Mamá must have done something similar after she tore up the letter for the first time.

I'm sure she had already learned to imitate Papá's handwriting, to recreate it on another piece of paper.

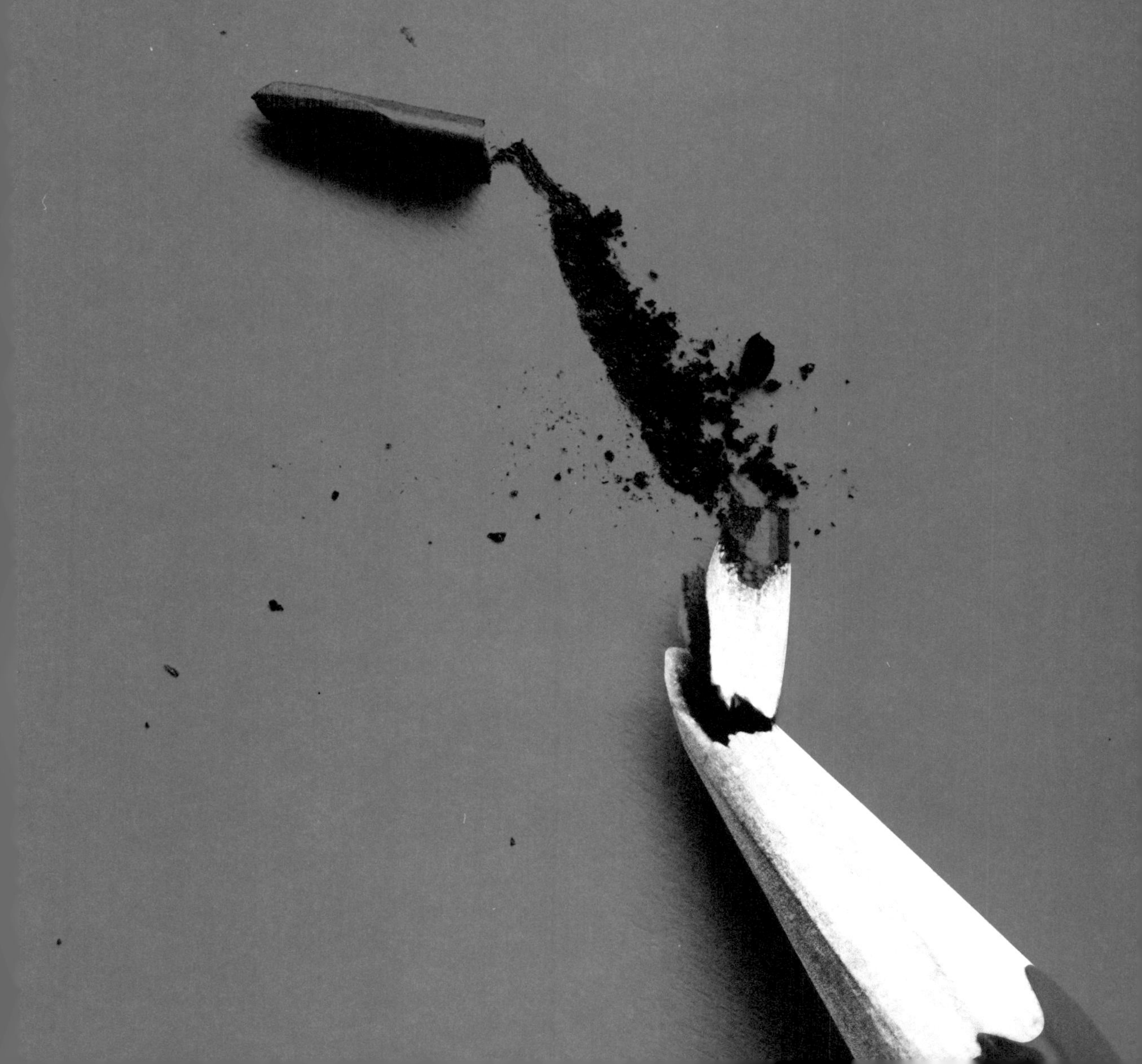

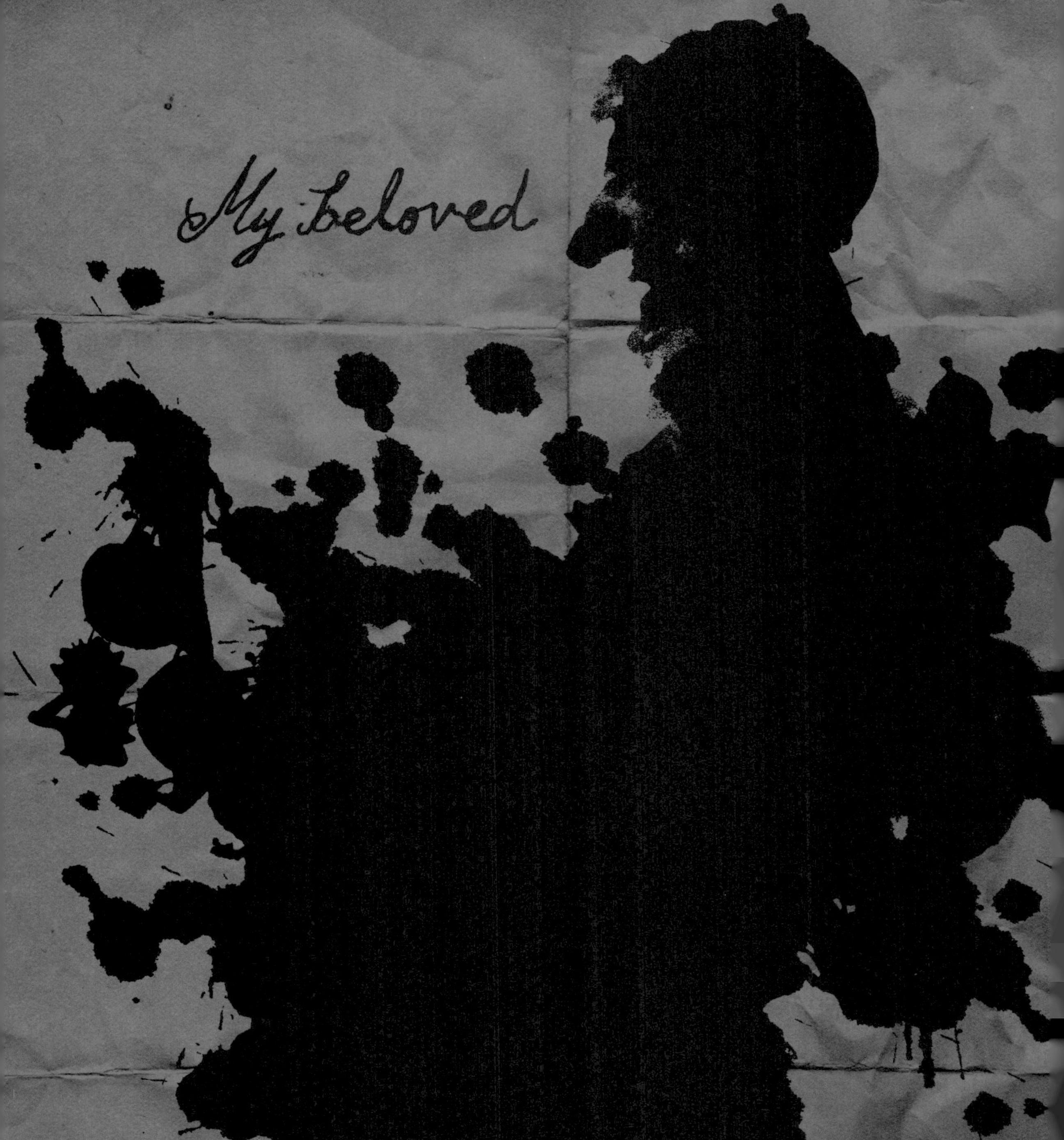
My beloved

That's how it begins, this letter that I've never read, because whenever I open the drawer and start to unfold it, my father always appears.

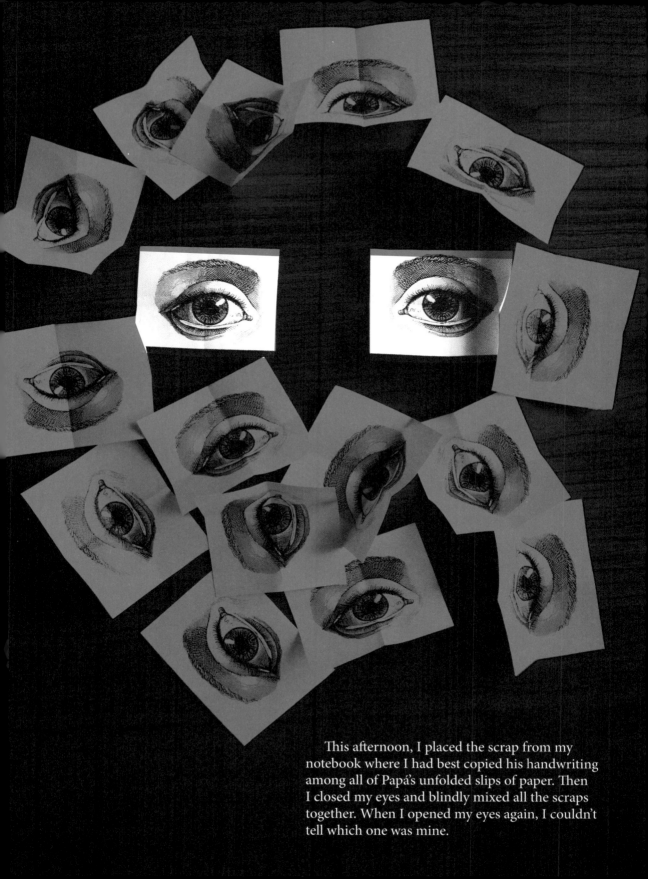

This afternoon, I placed the scrap from my notebook where I had best copied his handwriting among all of Papá's unfolded slips of paper. Then I closed my eyes and blindly mixed all the scraps together. When I opened my eyes again, I couldn't tell which one was mine.

Mamá is sleeping upstairs; Papá has fallen asleep on the chair down here. The clock goes: *tick-tock, tick-tock.* My mind goes: *The Book of Denial, The Book of Denial.* I enter Papá's study, sit at his desk, pick up his fountain pen, and open the notebook.

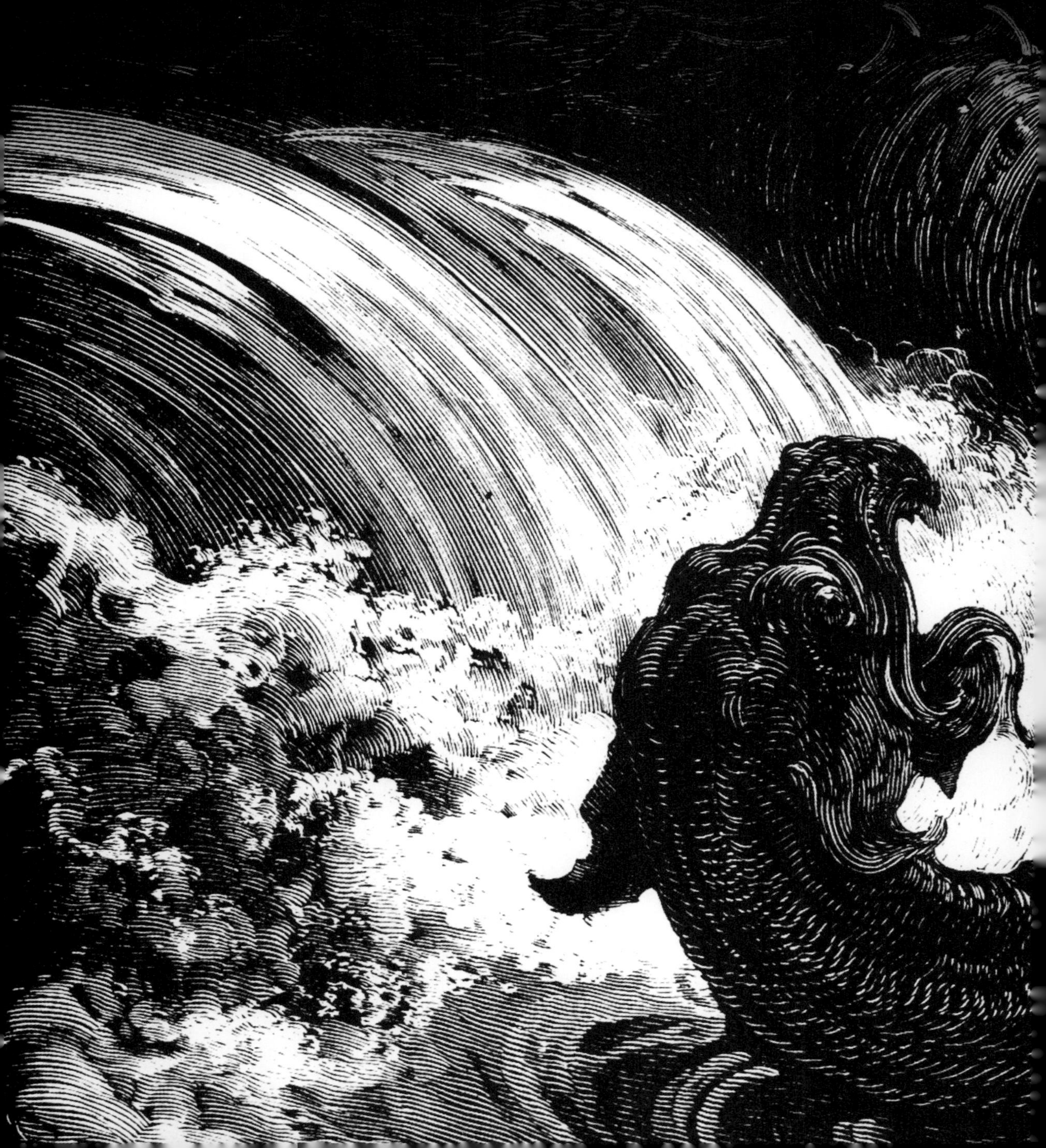

I see all the pages filled with his writing and think, *I've never written words that could not be erased later.*

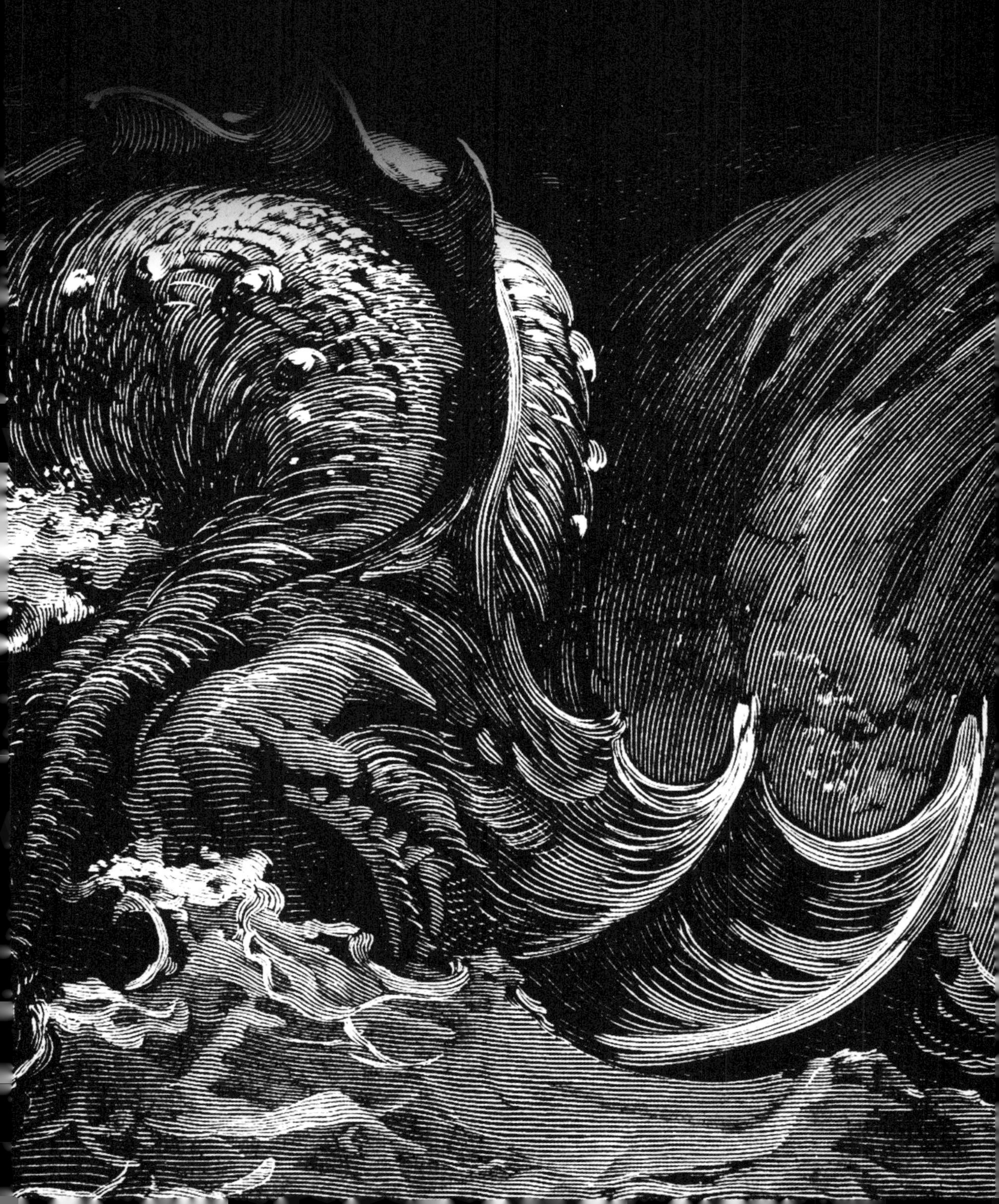

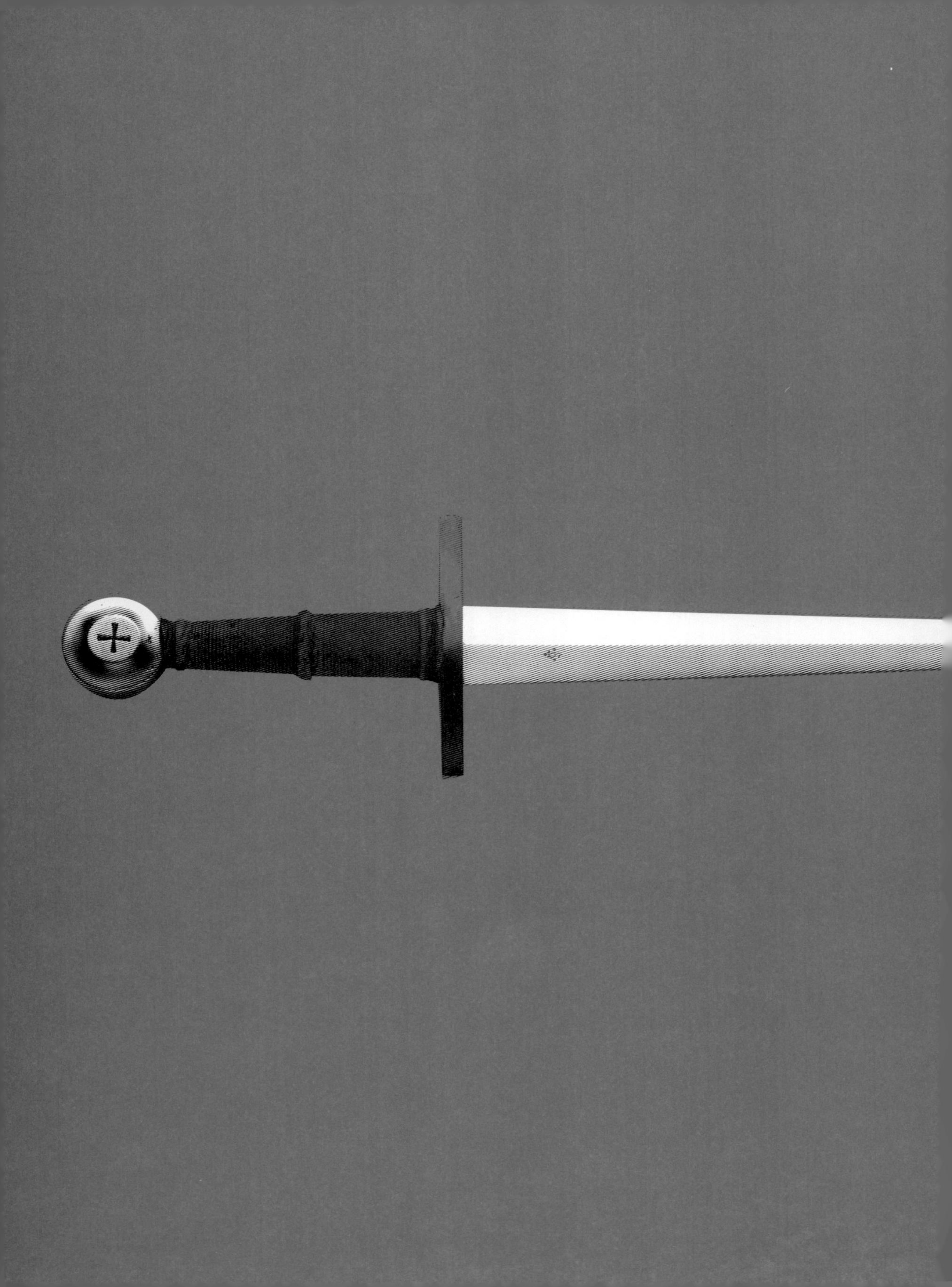

I begin not on the first page, but on one from the middle, chosen at random. It's the story in which the Roman emperor Nero has just killed his own mother.

To express their repudiation of a son doing something like that to his own mother, the Romans mounted a political protest that beggars belief: As if one abominable act demanded an even more wicked response, one thousand newborn babies were abandoned on the streets of Rome.
They were left there to die.

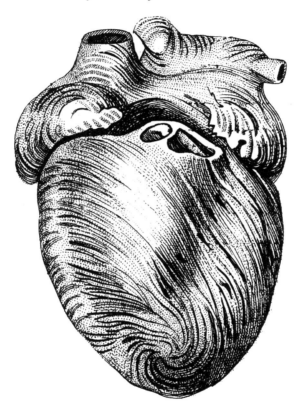

My hand trembled when I rested the pen on the paper.
I couldn't help but wonder if Mamá also took this long before breathing again.
If her vision also blurred when she finished writing.
When I let go of the fountain pen, everything was blurry: the bookcase,
Papá's diplomas on the wall, my own hands.
After a while I could breathe again, and little by little, everything cleared.
I was able to read what I had done.
*As if one abominable act demanded an even more wicked response,
one thousand newborn babies were not abandoned on the streets of Rome.
They were not left there to die.*

That's why it's called *The Book of Denial.*

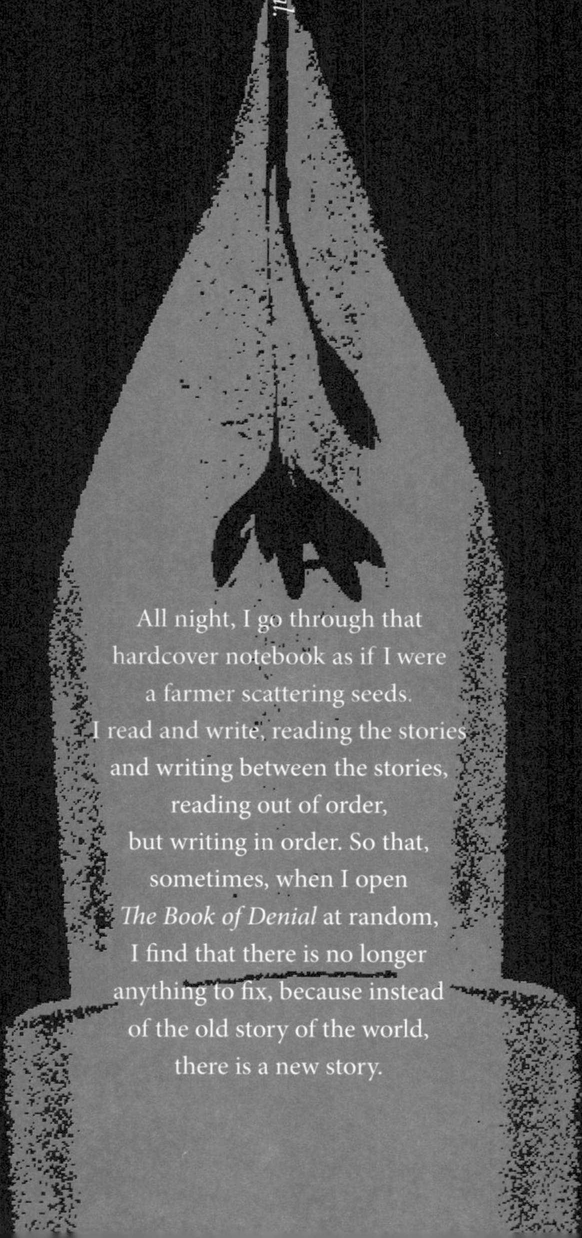

All night, I go through that
hardcover notebook as if I were
a farmer scattering seeds.
I read and write, reading the stories
and writing between the stories,
reading out of order,
but writing in order. So that,
sometimes, when I open
The Book of Denial at random,
I find that there is no longer
anything to fix, because instead
of the old story of the world,
there is a new story.

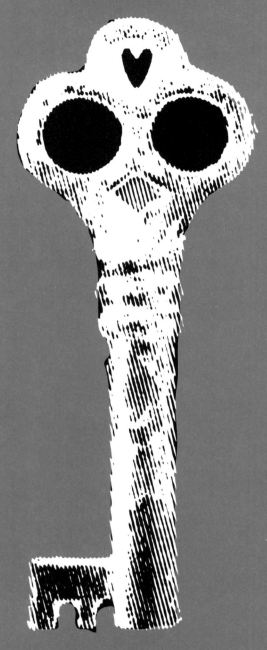

... these men did not scour the streets—did not kick open the doors of homes, did not search under the furniture, inside chests, behind the clothes, any place where a child under two could be hidden—and did not seize any infant they found with their two bare hands. Then, with those same naked hands, they did not put an end to them.

In Papá's handwriting, I write those letters of denial, tilted as if by the wind and undulating like waves, to change all of history, even if others don't care.

So long as we still care, right, Papá?

As it starts to grow light, I find that I've finished.

What *The Book of Denial* says now—as dawn and birdsong slip into the study—is that the ancient skulls of children in the sealed tomb were not full of holes, and that hundreds of thousands of children did not cross Europe and did not head to the shores of any sea; that the children of Basil were not beaten, were not exiled; and that Napoleon did not send hundreds and hundreds of children who could barely hold a weapon off to war.

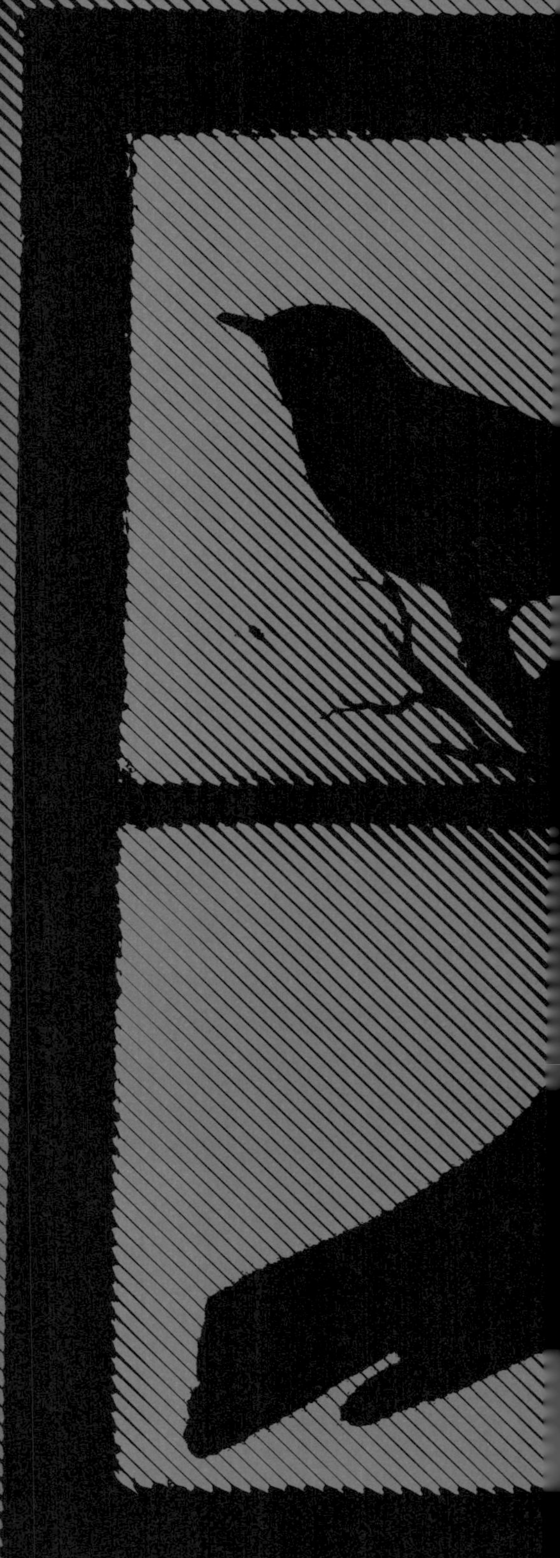

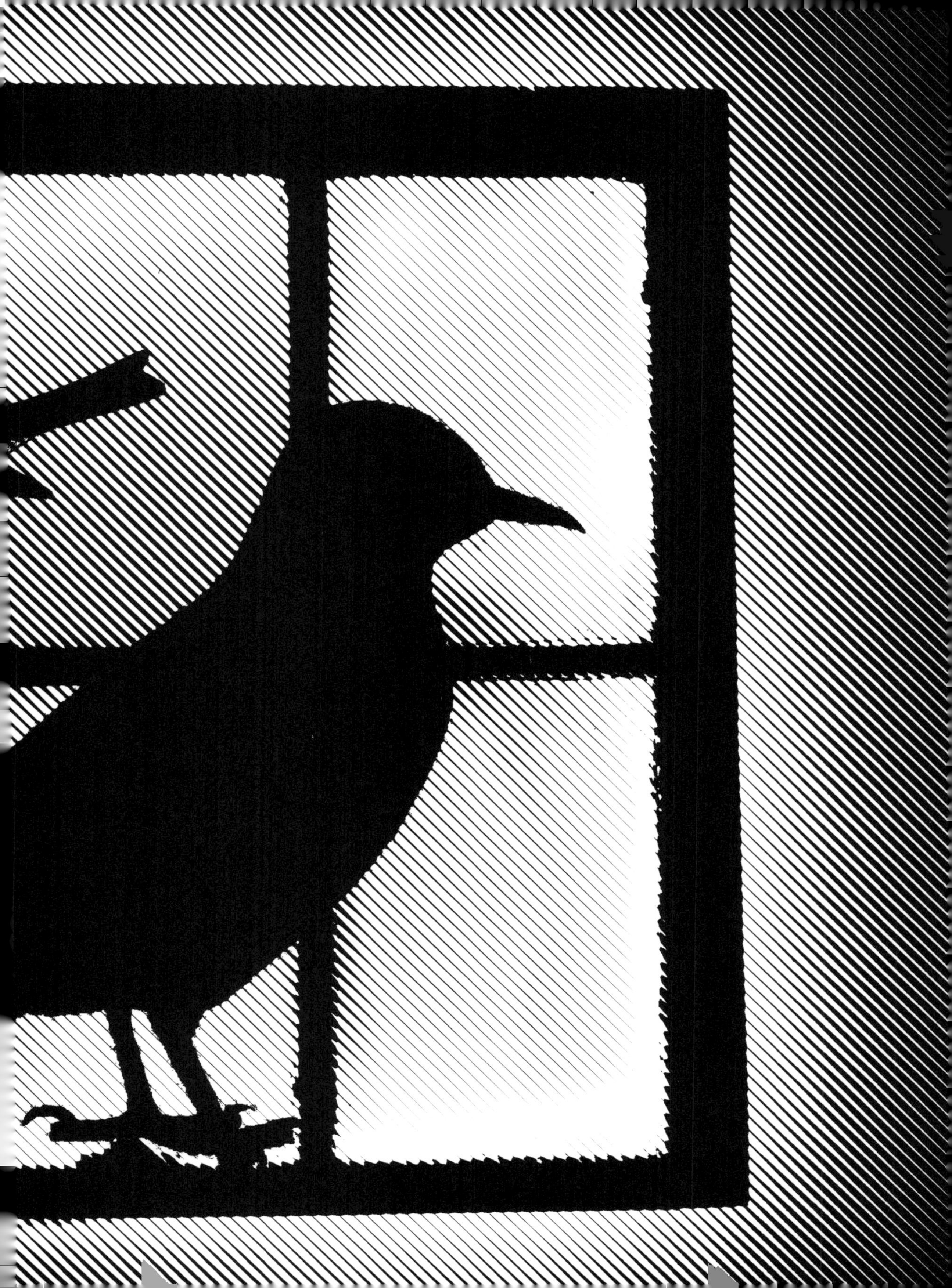

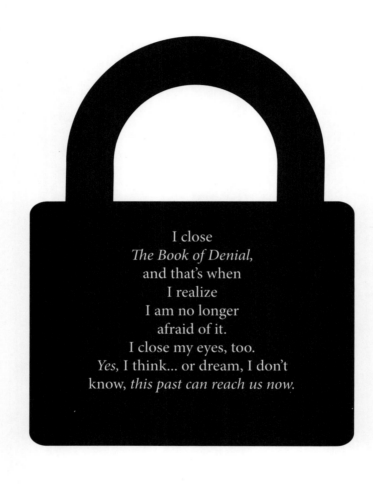

I close
The Book of Denial,
and that's when
I realize
I am no longer
afraid of it.
I close my eyes, too.
Yes, I think... or dream, I don't
know, *this past can reach us now.*

(The happy ending of the story)

THE STA
THE UN
ENDINC

Those who don't

wish to suffer

should not continue.

Because...

How can you see letters
without wanting to read them?

How can you look at the sea
without wanting to swim in it?

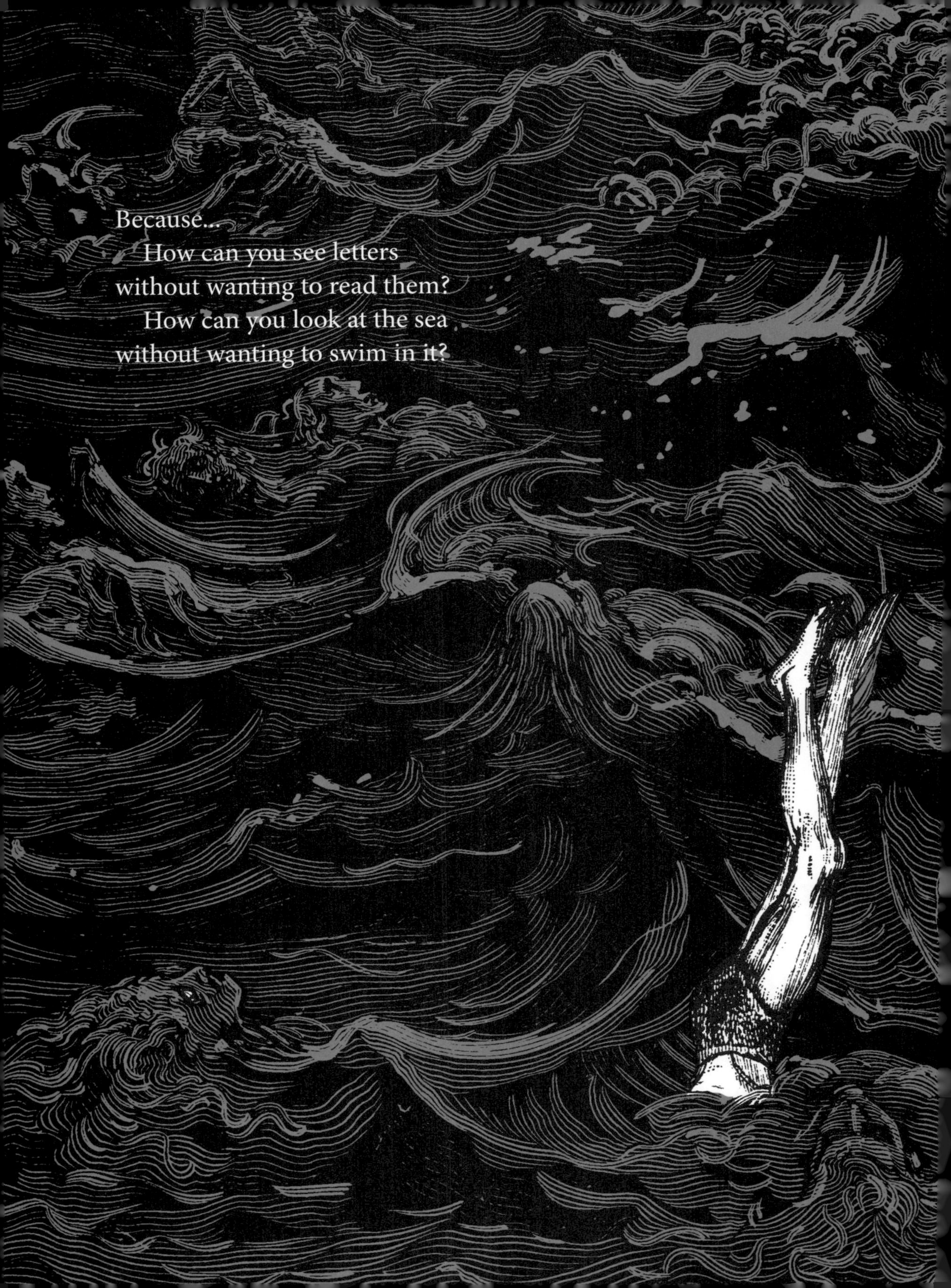

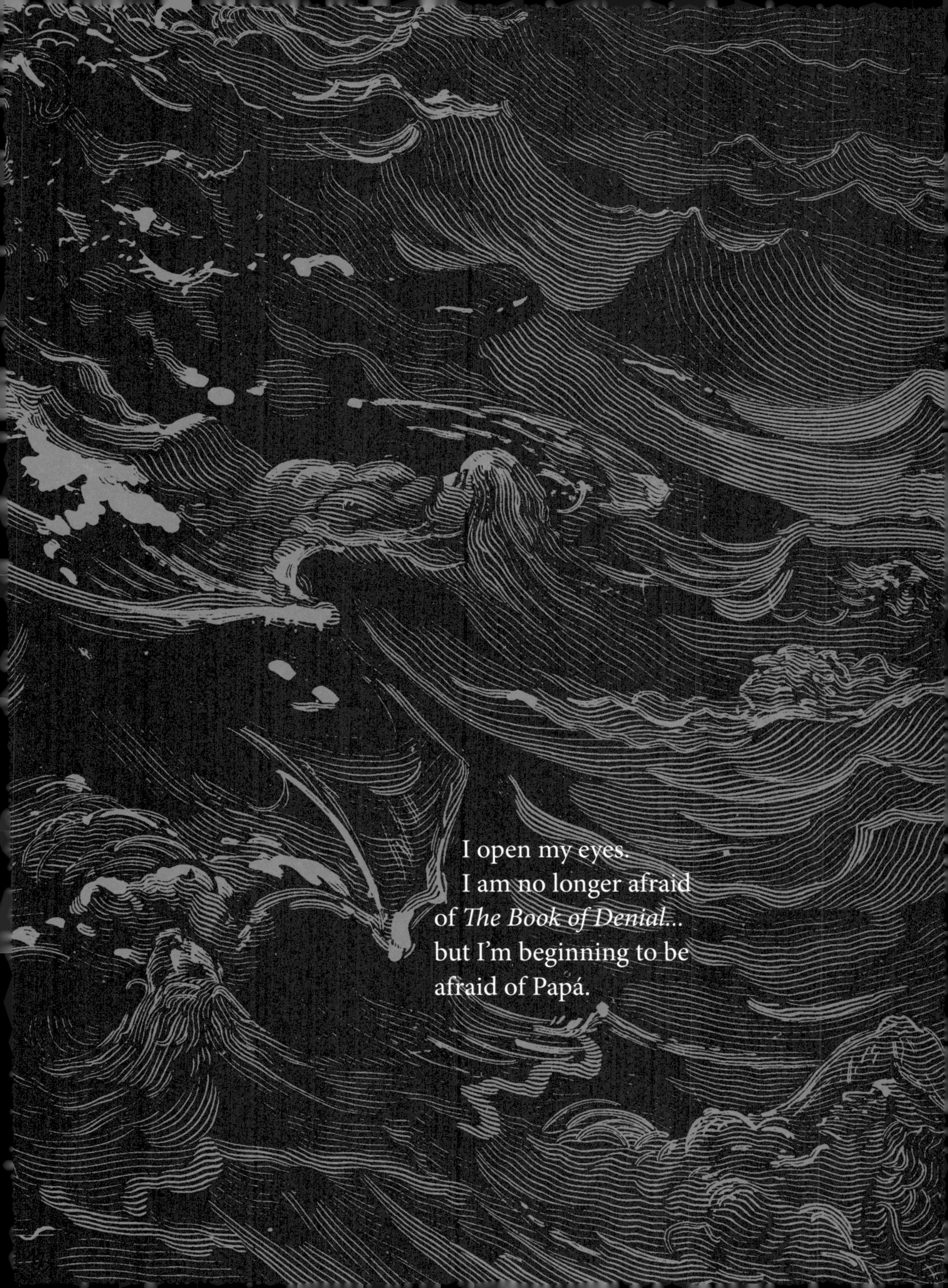

I open my eyes.
I am no longer afraid
of *The Book of Denial*...
but I'm beginning to be
afraid of Papá.

a b k l t h y u v o p w m a b g e f g m n j k l e r t y i o i

m n v b c h f h j k l o i u y f d s a y r e l k j h g f u y r e

a e I s l i p f r o m t h e s t u d y a q r e z m w x f c g

h n v e r y c a r e f u l l y , t h y k f a b c m n k l a d e i

w i t h o u t m a k i n g a s o u n d , a r w e r f g u i m

t x b u t P a p á i s n o l o n g e r k t u s p l u w p r g l

z o a s l e e p i n t h e l i v i n g r o o m . p l k a b c s

a g f d n m b n c v l k j h f i u y g f d s a y t l k j f s a e i

l k j h f i u y g f d m a b g e f g m n f d n m b t y i o i l r

z x c v f g h a e i k l o j h g f d y t r k m n l k j i a e m n

e i a o m n h g a p n b c f s a v d s d s f a e w z x t h m g

g h j i b v c g d f e s a i h g f a e l m n b o q f b f d d s a

l b v c g d f e s a i h e f g m n f d n m b t y i o i l j h g r

w p m n v b c h f g a p n b c f s a y r e l k j h g f u y r e i

s a x c v f g h a e i k l o j h f g h a e i k l o l k j i a t r n

l k a b c d e g p o d f h g f b b c t r e s s r s m v s a e c t

i o p d g f d z q w r b w r t y n l k j m n b v x a s w a e w

l j h g v x t r e d s a m n b v x z c v e w r t y a b i e a o l

h g f t r e a m n l o z x i w r y m n b c z g f s a t r e a l s

s a x c v f g h a e i k l o j h f g h a e i k l o l k j i a t r n l b v c g d f e s a i h e f g m n f d n m b t y i o i l j h g r

a g f d n m b n c v l k j h f i u y g f d s a y t l k j f s a e i

z f a M y t e a c h e r h a s e r a s e d z b v d s r w x f c g

g y a r v t h e 2 a n d t h e 9 n u w p r l k a a y r e l k j h

a s b f r o m t h e b l a c k b o a r d ; f d o d s a z a x d i

n t h e l a s t t h i n g I s e e u d s a n b a b t y l b v x z

x b e f o r e f a l l i n g a s l e e p d l k a d c t p l k j m n

k i s t h e n e w d a t e : k s p l u l g f w p r g l k a b c s

m l x O c t o b e r 3 0 . o u y f d s y r e l k j h g f u y r e

z x c v f g h a e i k l o j h g f d y t r k m n l k j i a e m n

g h j i b v c g d f e s a i h g f a e l m n b o q f b f d d s a

l k j h f i u y g f d m a b g e f g m n f d n m b t y i o i l r

w p m n v b c h f g a p n b c f s a y r e l k j h g f u y r e i

s a x c v f g h a e i k l o j h f g h a e i k l o l k j i a t r n

h g f t r e a m n l o z x i w r y m n b c z g f s a t r e a l s

l j h g v x t r e d s a m n b v x z c v e w r t y a b i e a o l

a b k l t h y u v o p w m a b g e f g m n j k l e r t y i o i

i o p d g f d z q w r b w r t y n l k j m n b v x a s w a e w

l k a b c d e g p o d f h g f b b c t r e s s r s m v s a e c t

e i a o m n h g a p n b c f s a v d s d s f a e w z x t h m g

What I think as I'm leaving school,
so I won't be afraid anymore,
is that it's been a long time since Papá hit me.

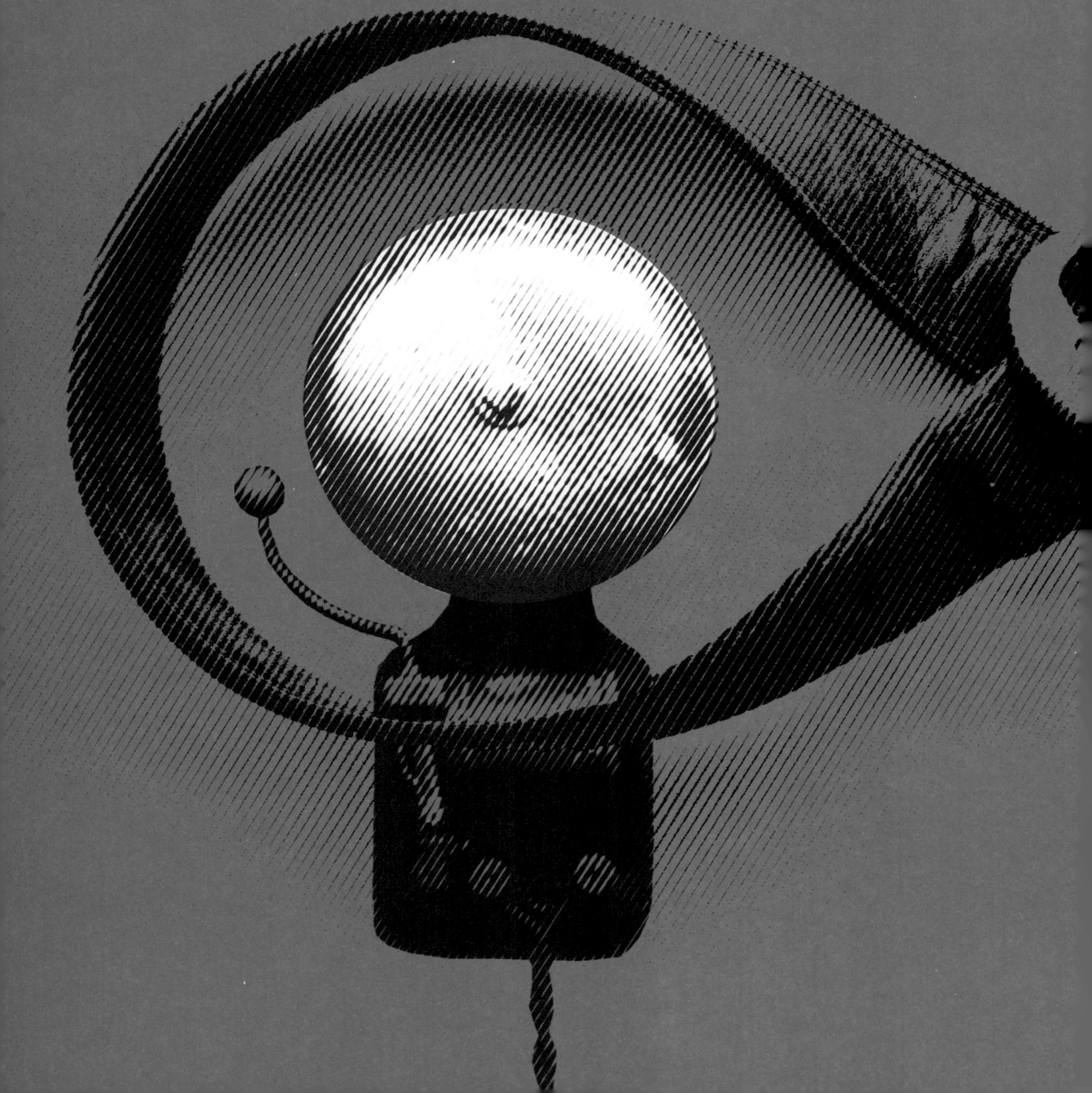

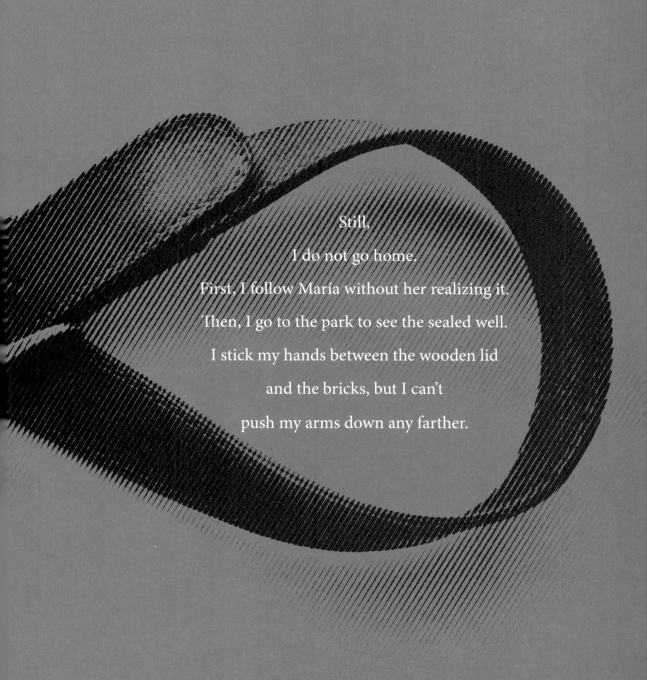

Still,

I do not go home.

First, I follow María without her realizing it.

Then, I go to the park to see the sealed well.

I stick my hands between the wooden lid

and the bricks, but I can't

push my arms down any farther.

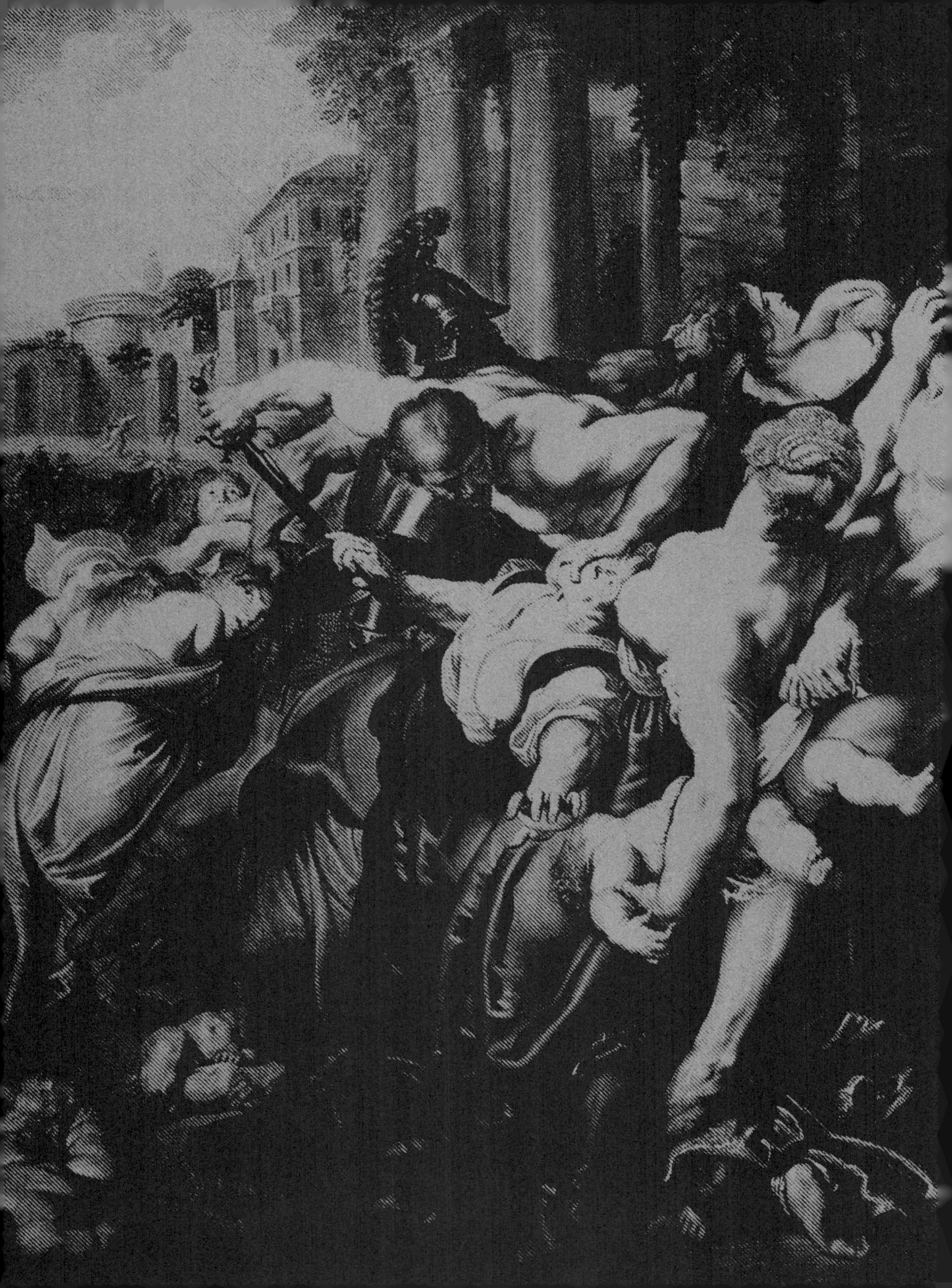

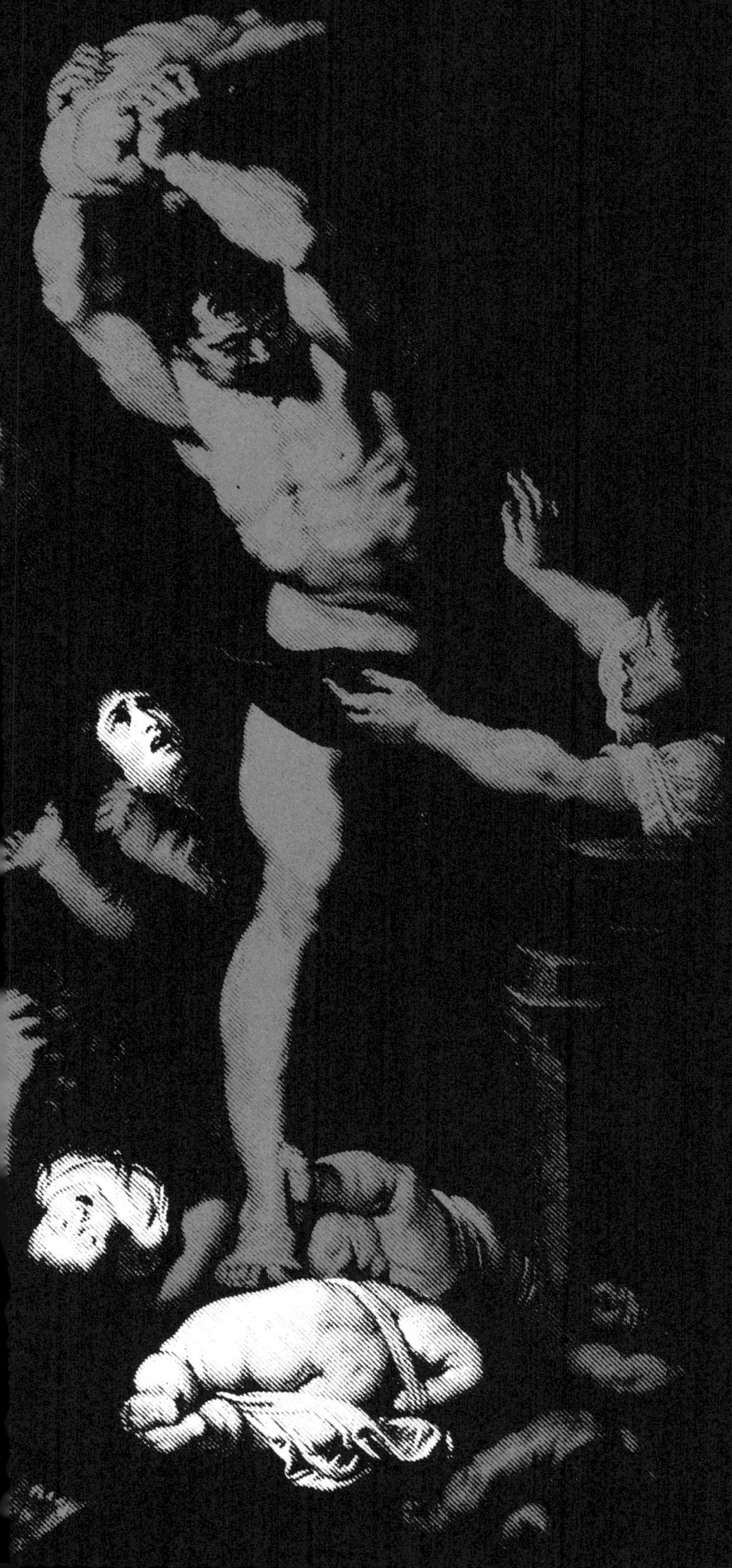

"Why didn't they run away?"

Isn't that what one of my classmates asked when we talked about the Holy Innocents?

I would tell him that it would not have been enough for the babies to know how to walk, to know how to run, to know that they felt afraid.

I would even answer them with other questions:

"Why didn't all the children who were killed run away, then?"

"Did they say something wrong?"

And...

"How could they have defended themselves?"

And...

"Did they know what was going to happen?"

And...

"How could the adults declare war against children?"

That's what I would ask my classmates.

And I would tell them to shut up.

"Shut up! Shut up... if you don't know what you're talking about!"

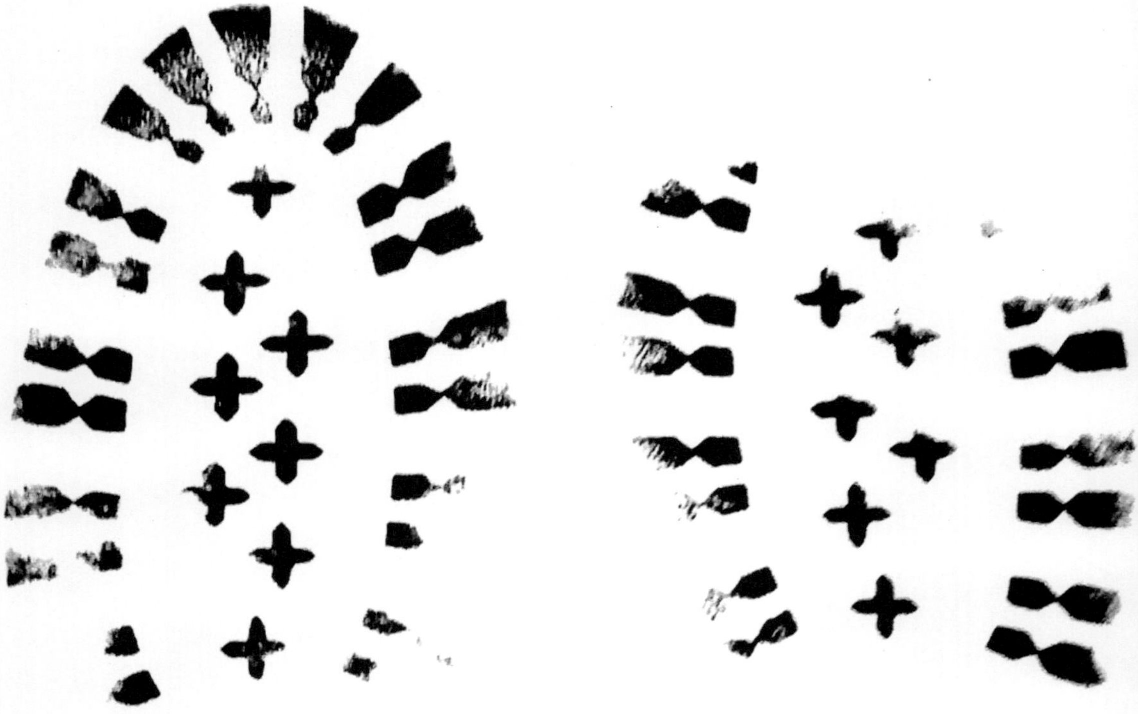

The worst thing of all is discovering that while all paths lead far from home, the only path we really know is the one that leads us back.

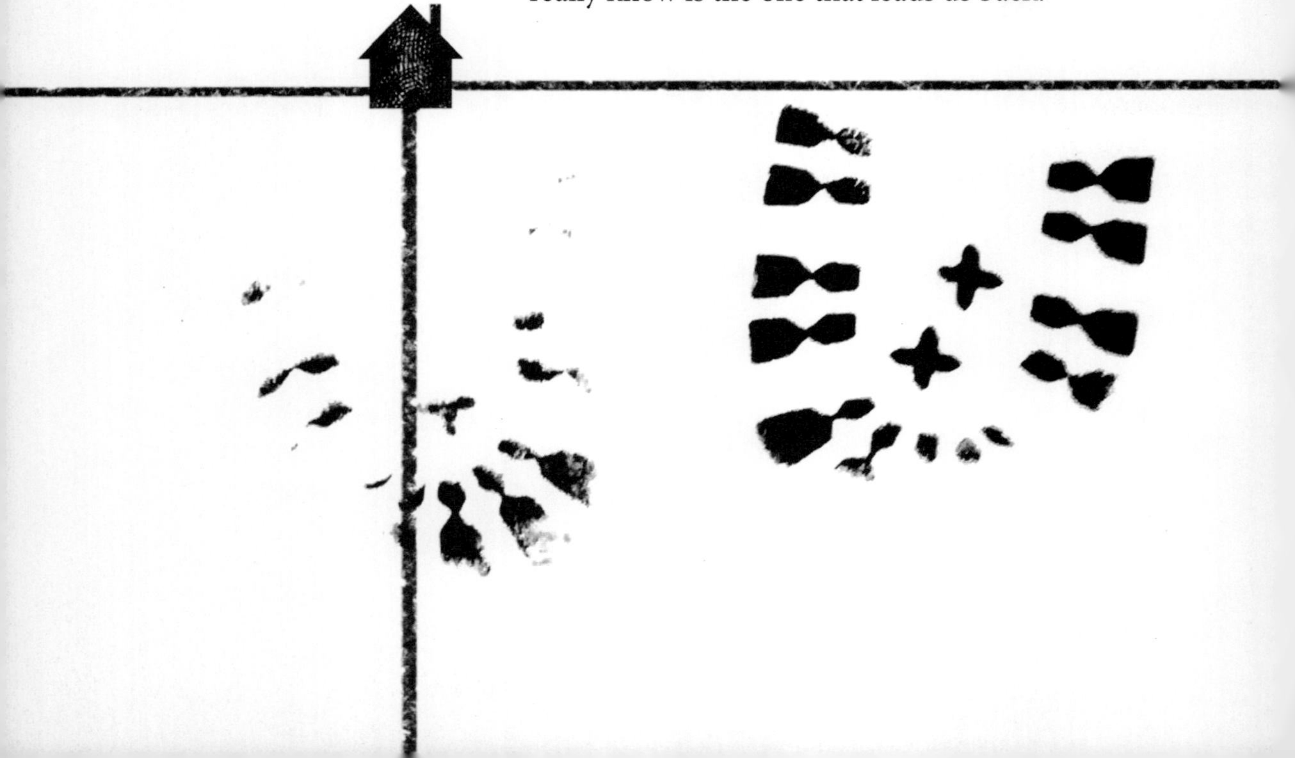

Are we at war, Papá?

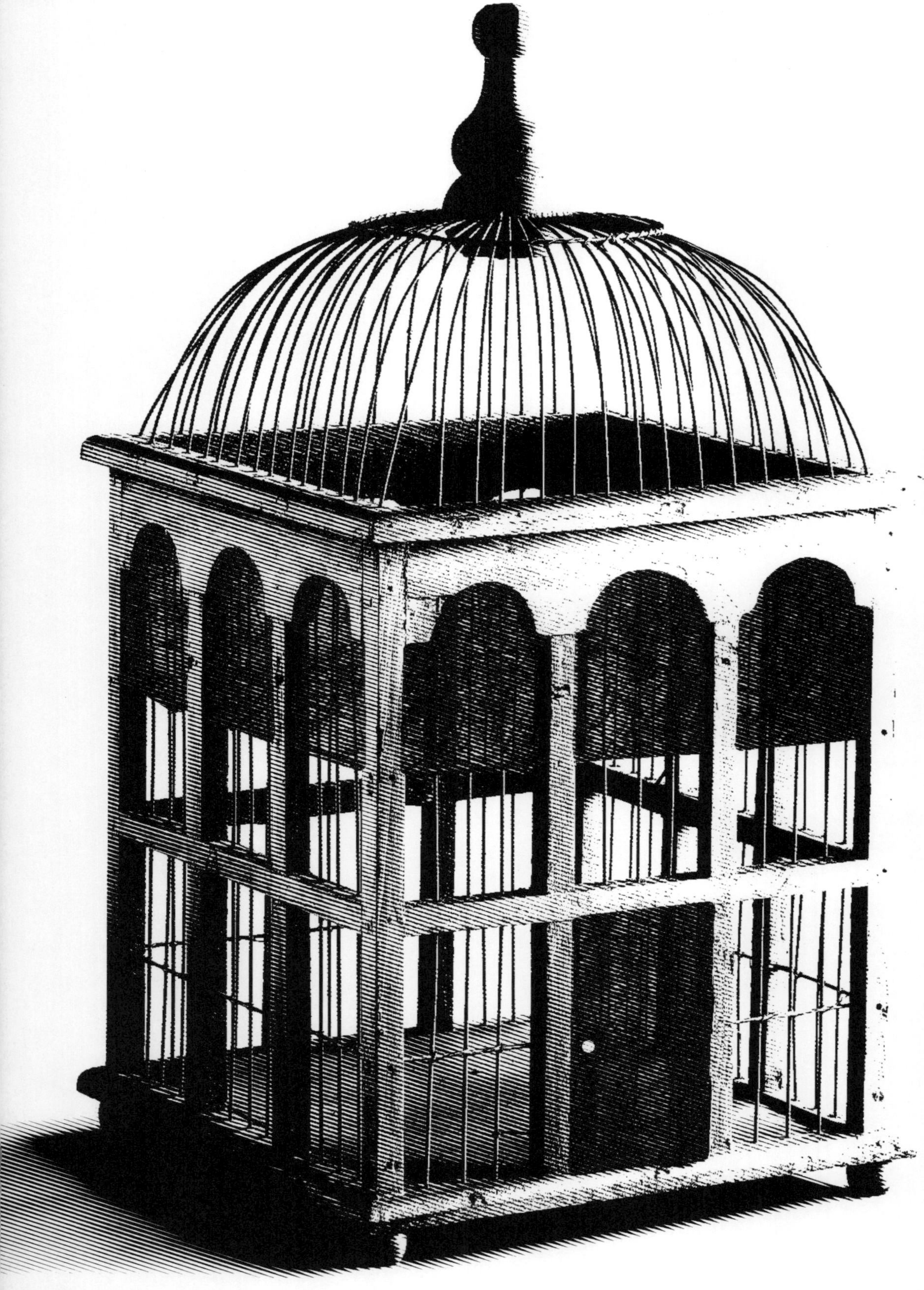

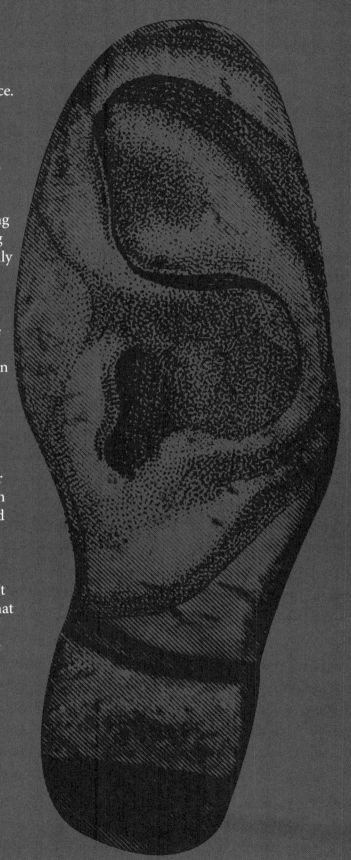

The house is filled with shadows and silence.

The table is set as usual, with three plates and three napkins and three sets of silverware.

Papá is not in the garden, not in the kitchen, not in the living room, not in the dining room. And upstairs, only Mamá is asleep.

The door to the study.

I approach on tiptoe to look through the keyhole, and that's when the voice from within booms:

"ENTER."

Then I don't hear anything anymore.

I don't hear the door when I open it, or when it closes by itself behind me. I don't hear my steps as I walk toward the seat that is beside my father's chair. I don't even hear the moans that I feel escape from my chest as I sit down. The only thing I hear is the deafening buzz inside my head. I can't even hear myself think.

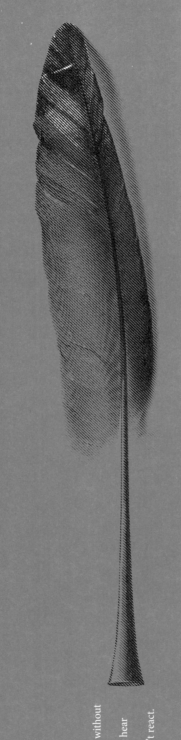

"Papá," I whisper without hearing myself. Maybe he doesn't hear anything either, because he doesn't react.

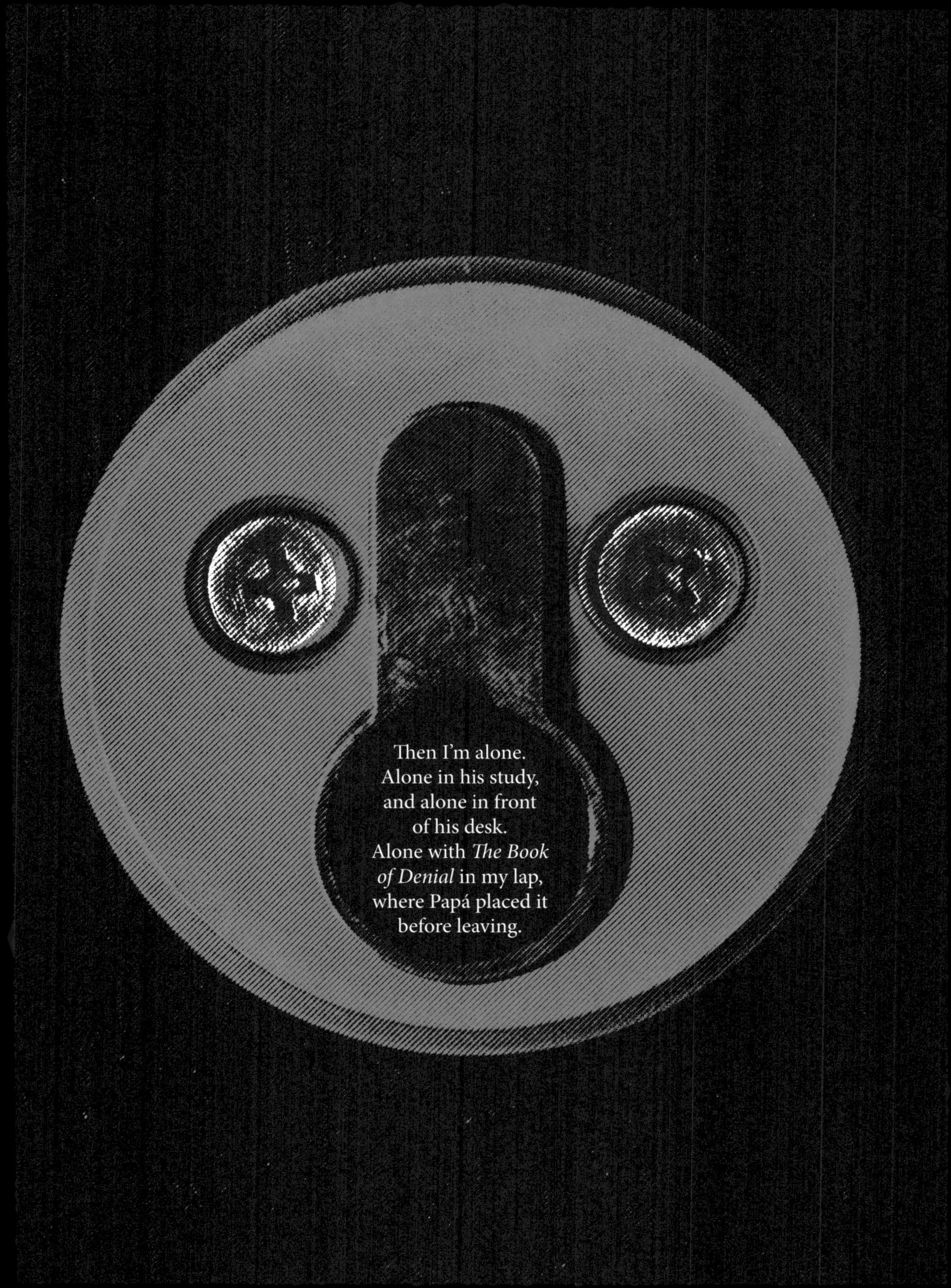

Then I'm alone.
Alone in his study,
and alone in front
of his desk.
Alone with *The Book
of Denial* in my lap,
where Papá placed it
before leaving.

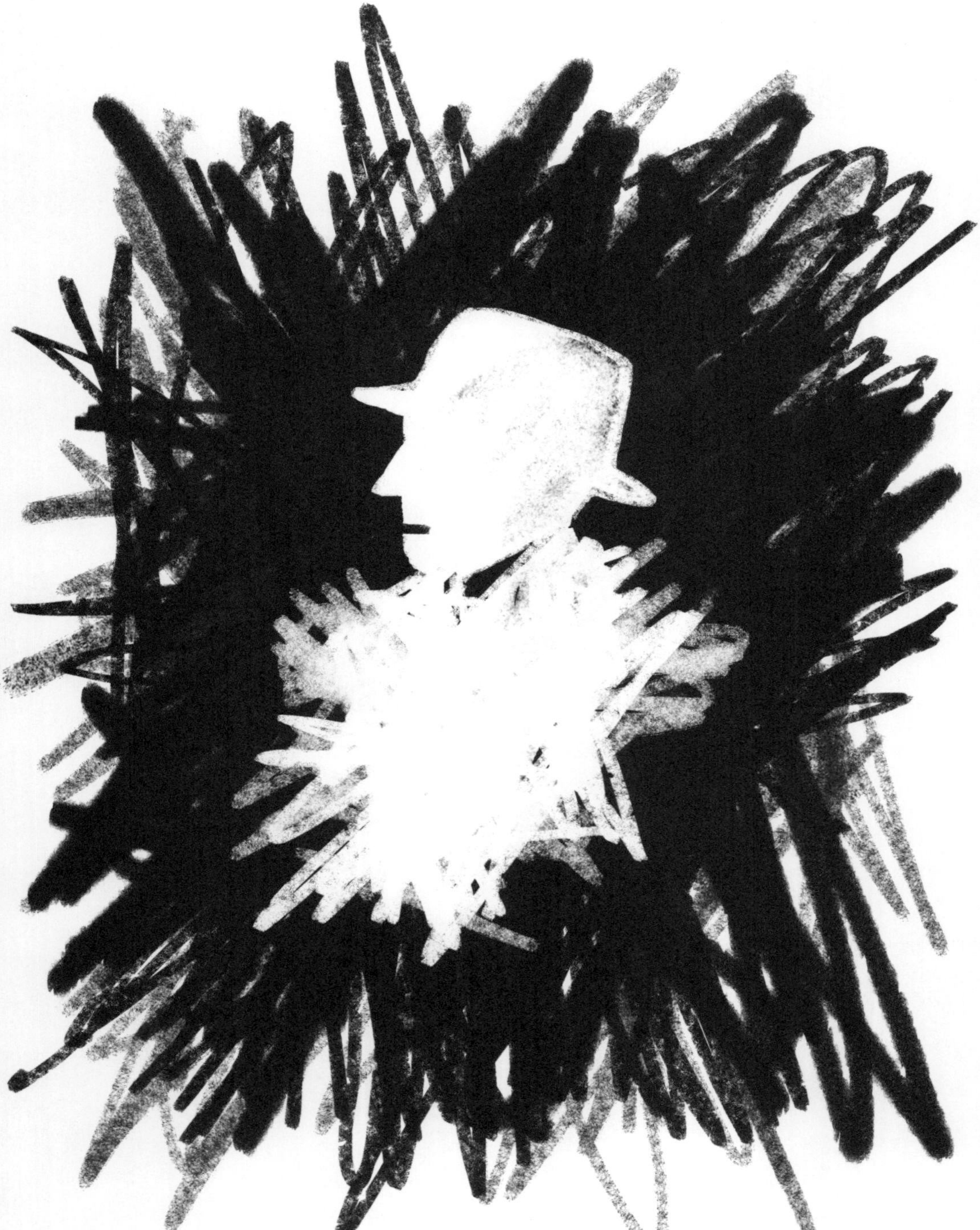

For a long time, I don't move.

I don't dare to get up; I don't dare to open the notebook; I don't dare to look behind me to where Papá might be waiting. At some point, without realizing it, I've opened *The Book of Denial.* What I do realize is that inside, there are no words crossed out, no torn pages, nothing like that.

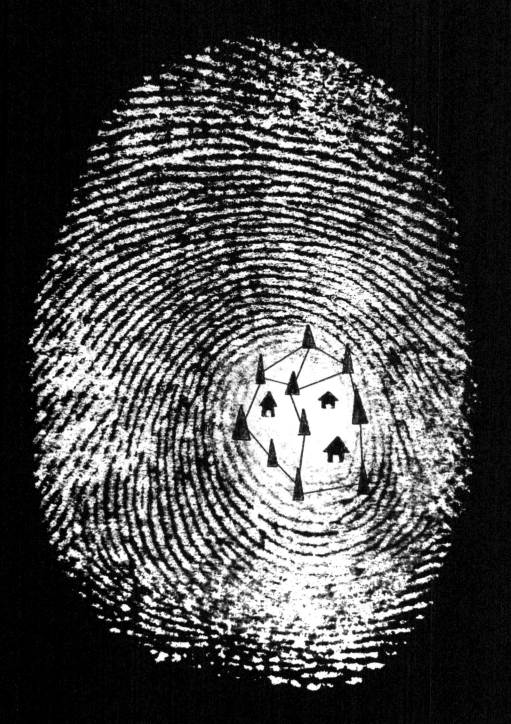

I concentrate on following those letters I wrote that so resemble Papá's. I fix my eyes on them as if they were tracks and I were lost in the forest. "Did not," "did not," "did not." I proceed from page to page until I've almost reached the end of the book. There, I find a few scraps of paper like the ones that once fell out of Papá's pocket.

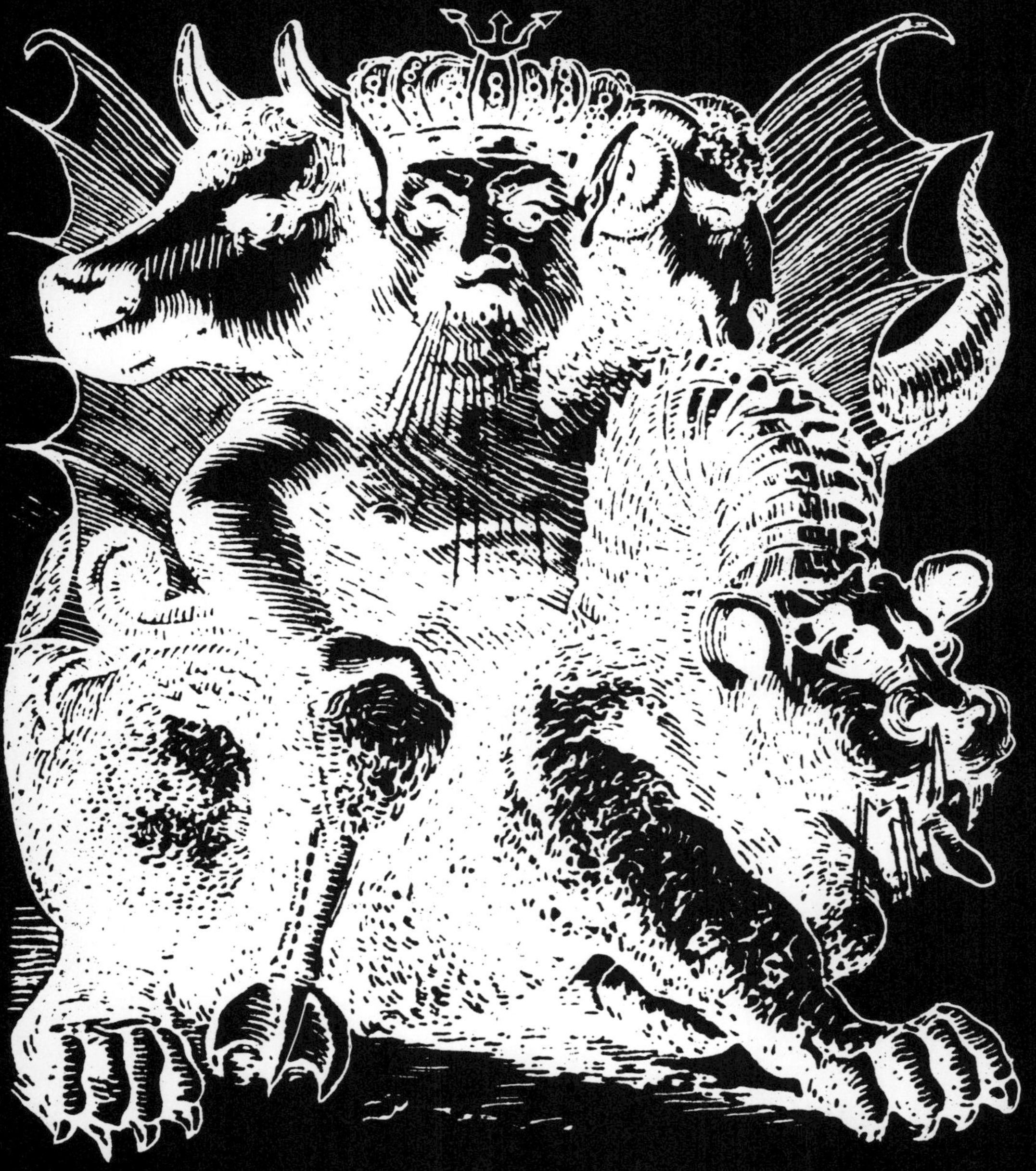

What I read with resignation, with sadness, as if I've always known it, is that the past has reached us:

Over the past ten years, ten million children have been killed around the world for the sake of a nation, a religion, an economy, a leader.
And on another scrap:
One million languish in orphanages.
And on another:
Ten million took part in wars.
And on another:
Three million girls and boys are victims of sexual exploitation.

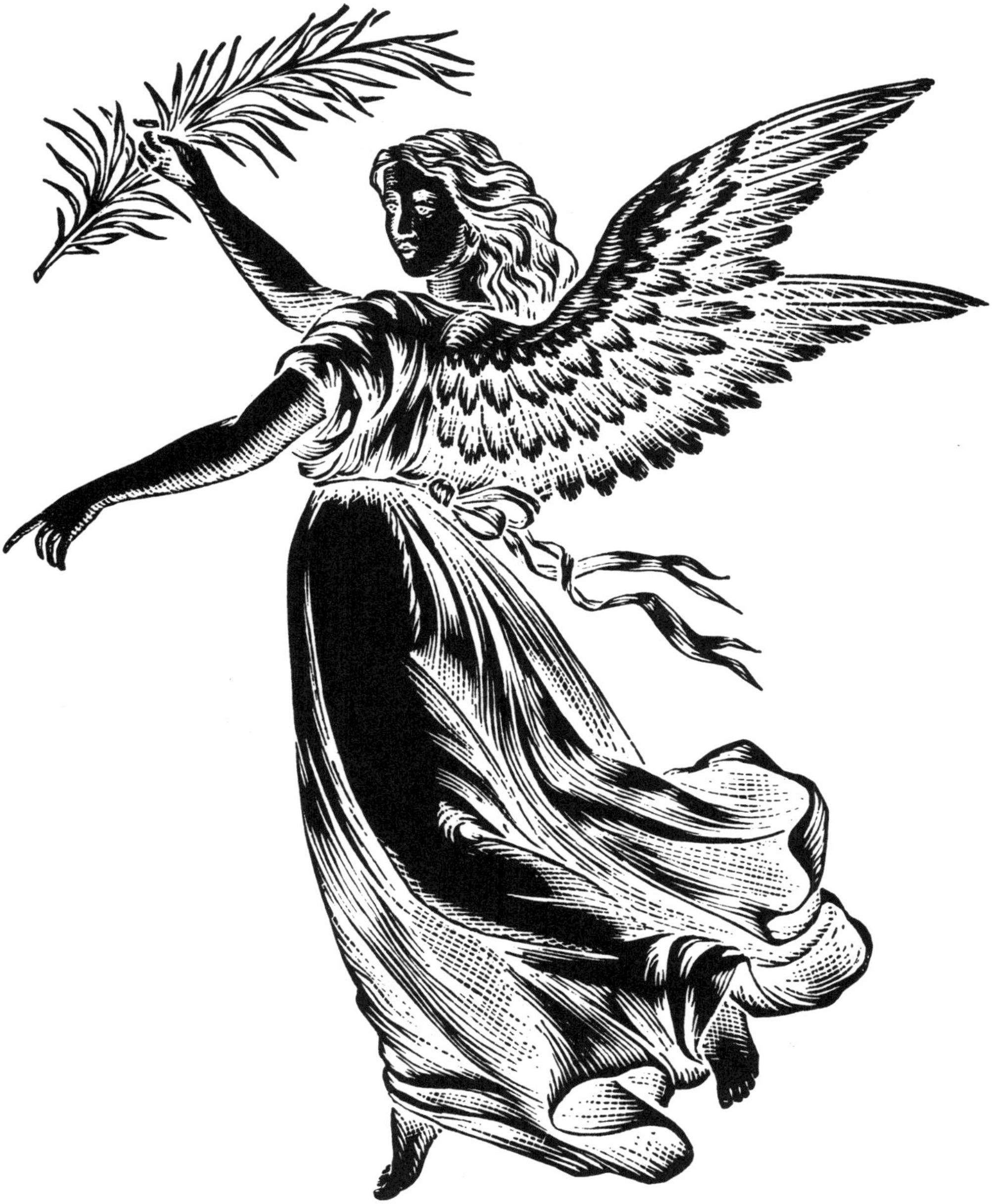

Then, one of the scraps accidentally slips from my hand, and I discover that there is also something written on the back.

Over the past ten years, ten million children have not been killed around the world for the sake of a nation, a religion, an economy, a leader.
I turn over another:
One million do not languish in orphanages.
And another:
Ten million did not take part in wars.
And another:
Three million girls and boys are not victims of sexual exploitation.

I practiced a lot to make my handwriting look like Papá's, but not so much that I managed to make the letters tilt just so.

My father's "nots" are so lovely. As lovely as a caress.

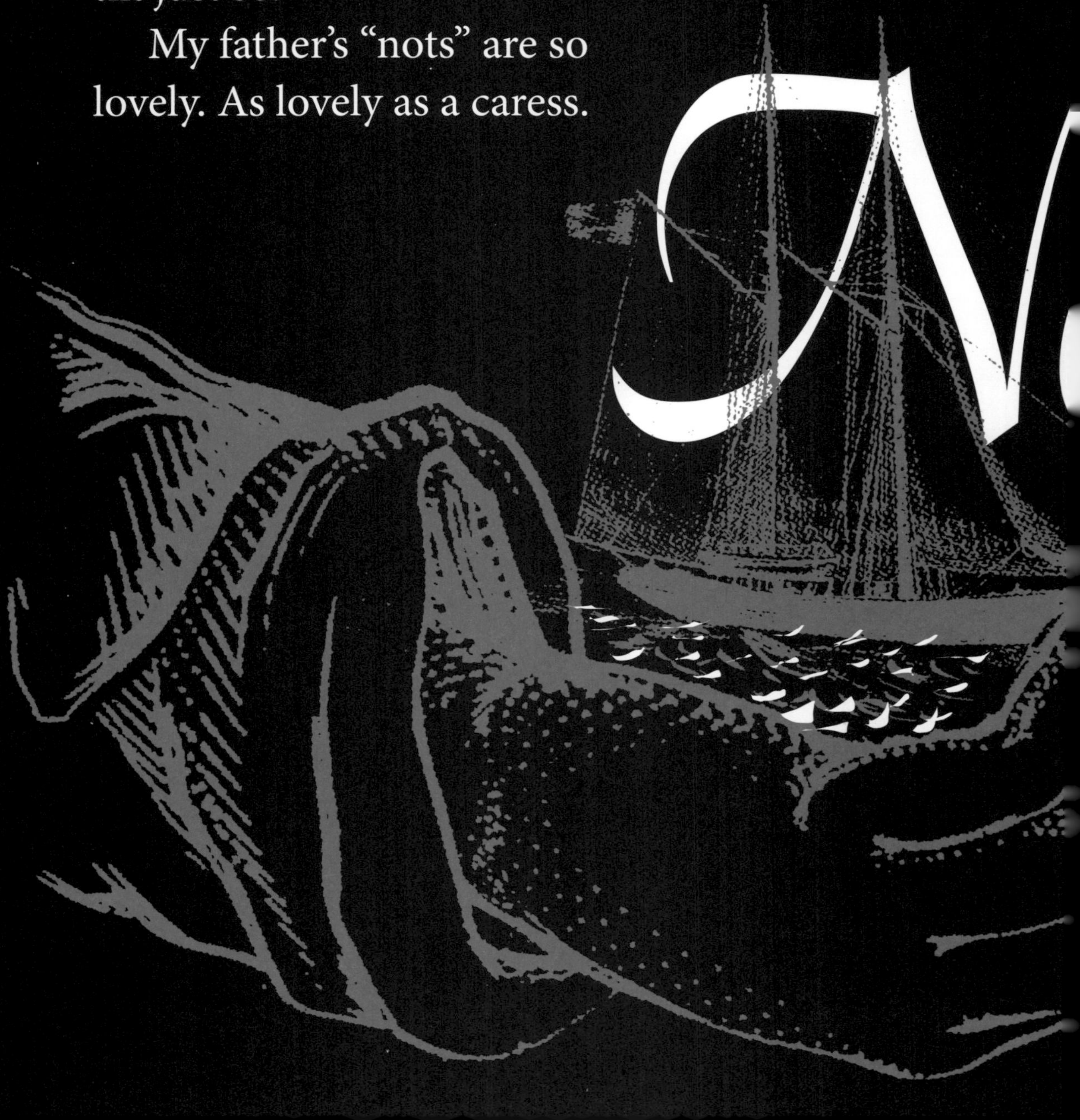

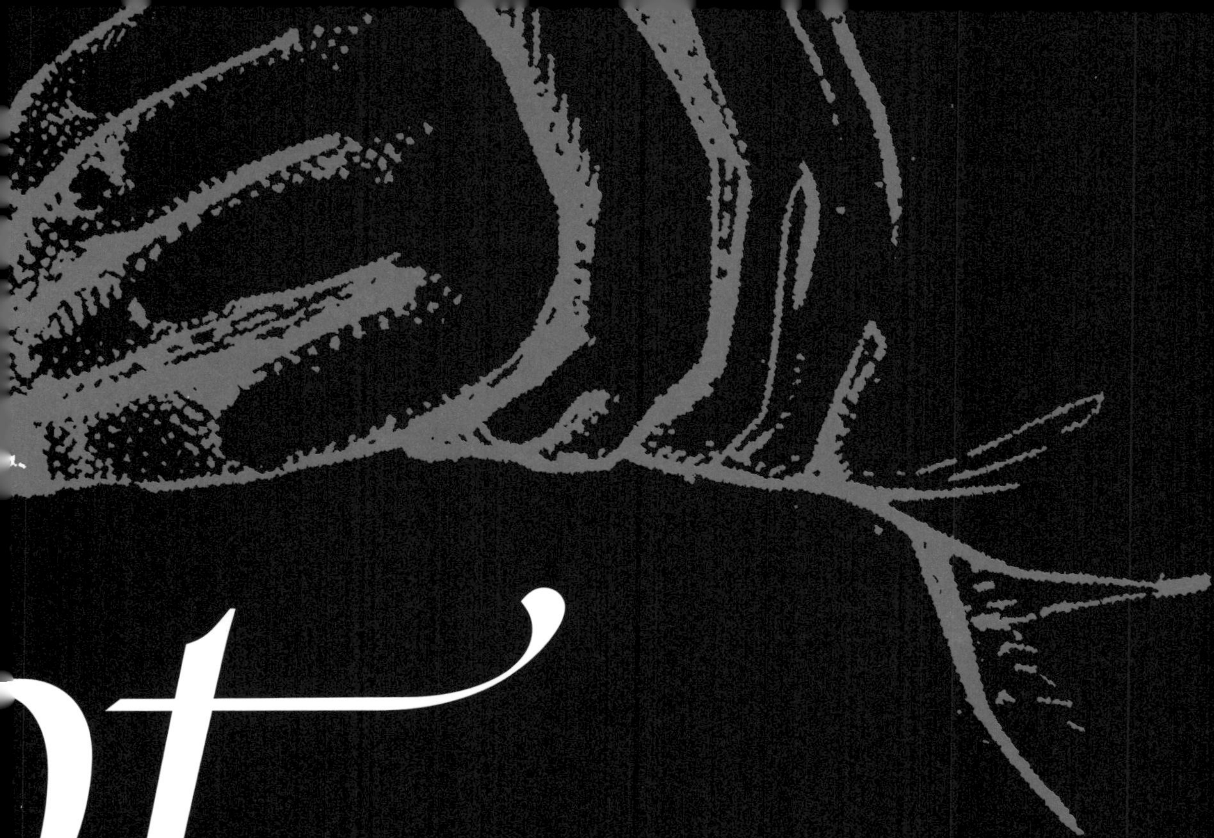

Then I discover something written on the next-to-last page of the notebook:

I wanted to write this book so that what we do to children never ceases to be a problem; to leave this human problem as a legacy to human reckoning; so that no one dares to forget a story that is not one of inhumanity, but of our most terrible humanity.
I wanted to bequeath this story of terror so that it would become a human topic that is always talked about, always thought about, always written about: love, death, sacrifice, sickness... the murder of children. So that people don't stop thinking about, talking about, and writing about this tragedy—not until word becomes deed, for only then can our worst history be changed. Only then can we put a definitive end to this unhappy ending.

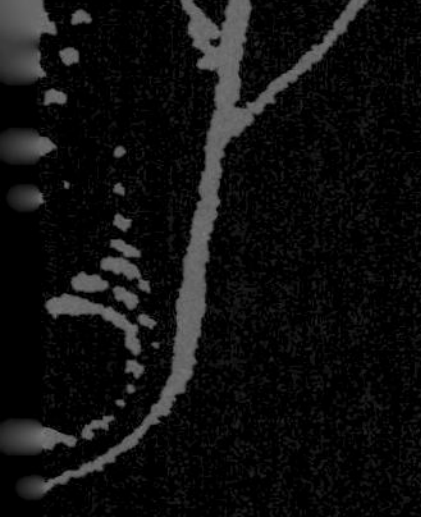

Then I come to the last page.

This is why I decided to dedicate this book to my son, and to my son's children, and to the children of my son's children.

But today, my son has shown me something that I never knew before. He has shown and given it to me: grace. The grace for me to inherit backward instead of forward.

The chance for me to make his gift reach back to my father, and from my father to my grandparents, and from my grandparents to my great-grandparents, and from my great-grandparents to all the ancestors of human history.

NOT.

That is the gift I've received from my son.

NOT.

So that it reaches all the way back to the beginning of the worst human story.

Instead of a happy ending, a happy beginning for the world's children, for all times.

The last page of the notebook is a calm sea
filling up with rain.

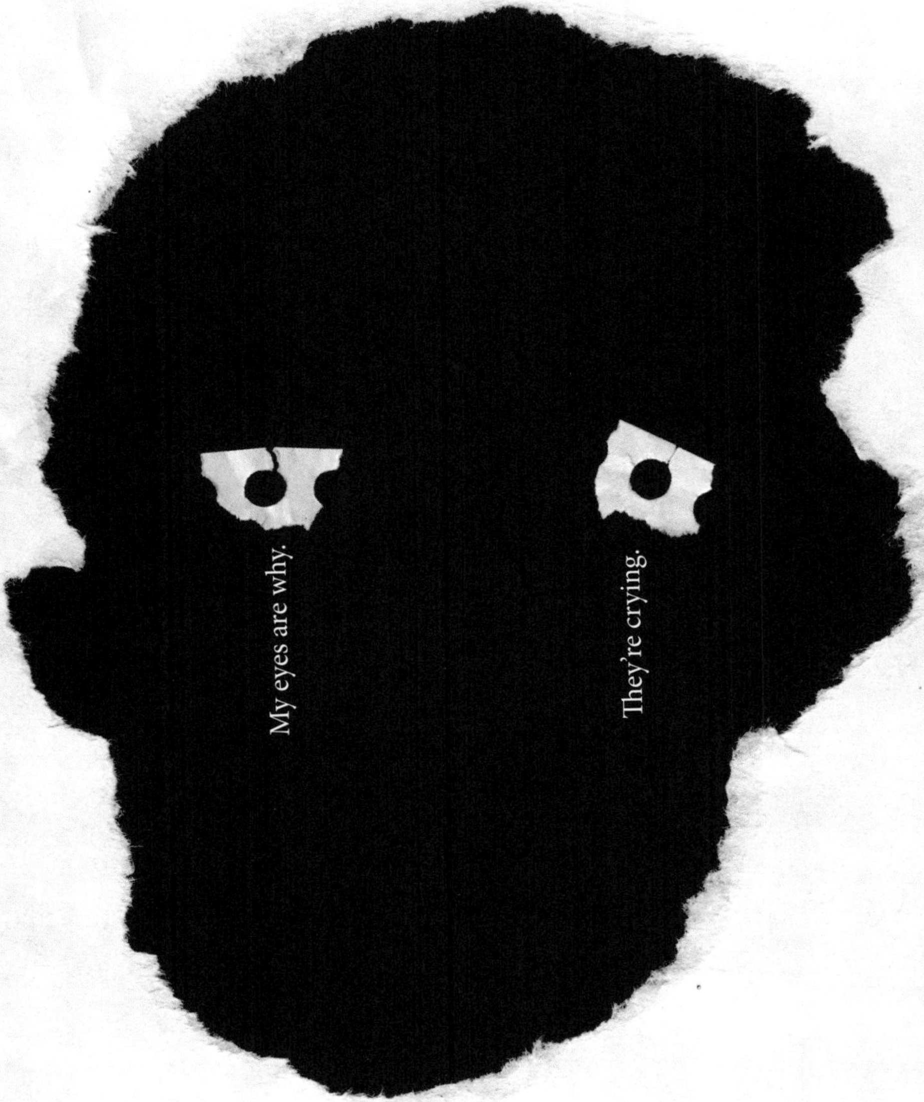
My eyes are why.
They’re crying.

On their own, without me or my lips, which I feel
curve into a smile, because Papá has never said
anything so beautiful to me before.

Before closing *~~The Book of Denial~~*, I discover that it's no longer called that. The title has been crossed out and now reads: *The Worst Book in the World.*

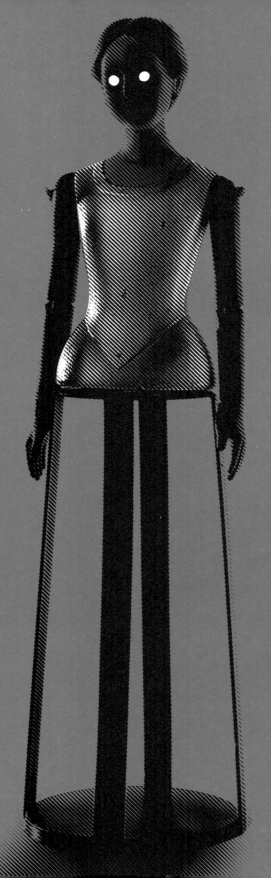

Today is November 1.
The Day of the Dead.
I don't go to school,
although there are classes.
Mamá doesn't stay in bed.
Papá stops wandering
and staring at his hands.
Instead, Mamá puts on
her best clothes.
Papá puts on his best clothes.
I put on my best clothes,
and we all go out together.

They each take one of my hands and we walk like this to the park, but then we keep on going. With me in the middle, and one of them on each side.

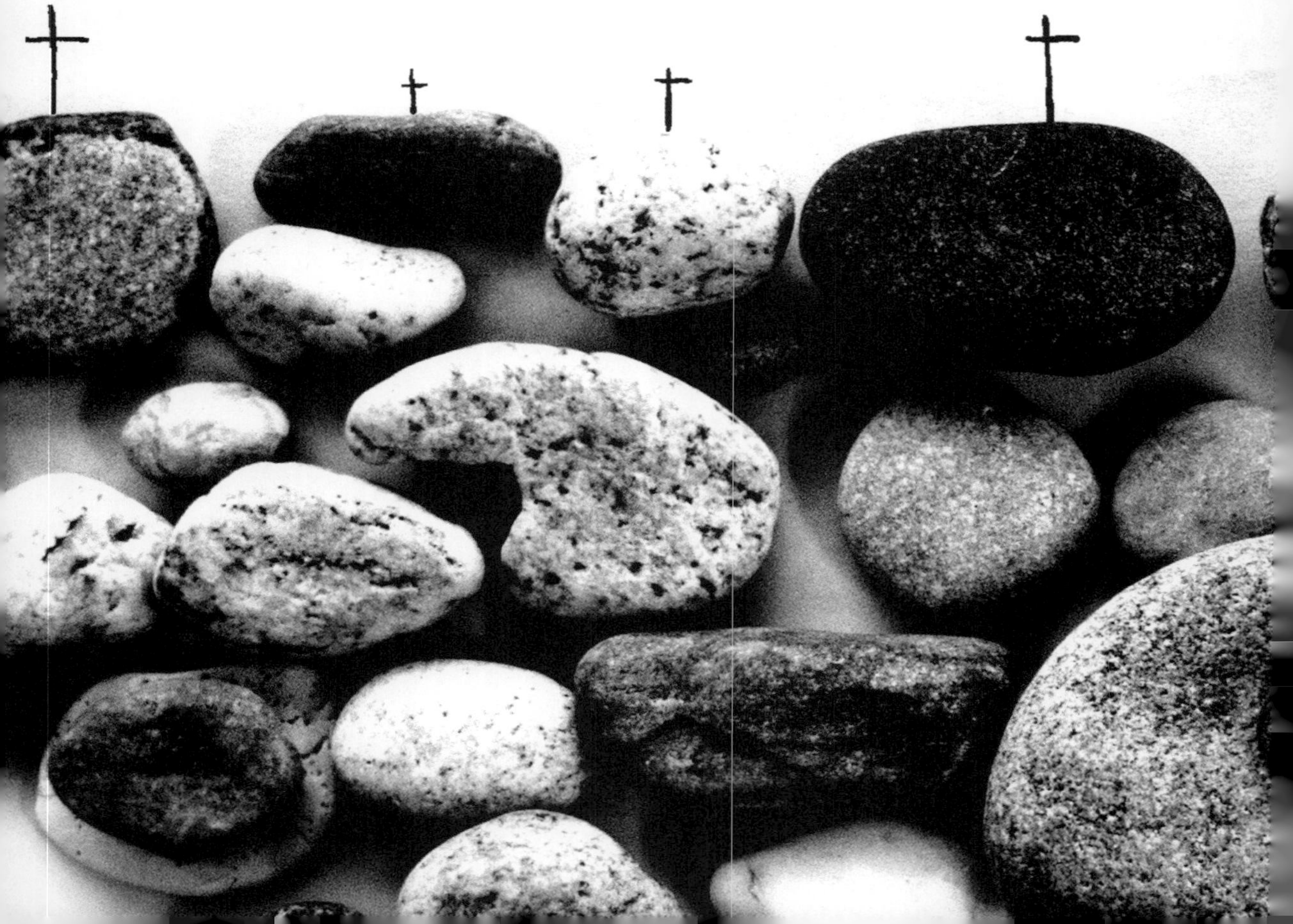

The cemetery of our city is like a green ocean, full of ships of white stone that don't move. A sea at peace.

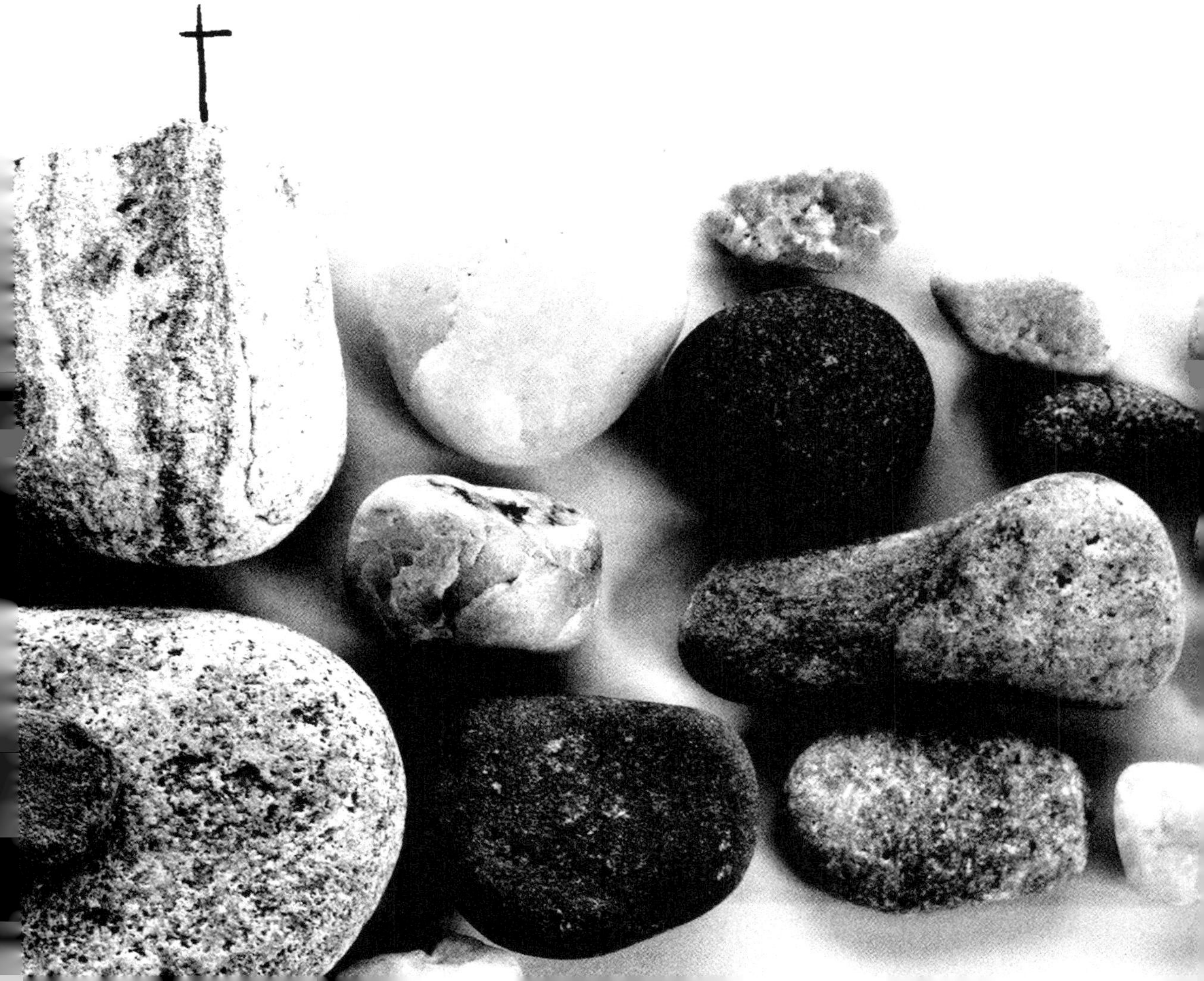

We're not the only ones who walk
upon the green waters of this still ocean.
Many people bring flowers, along
with grief and a sense of peace.

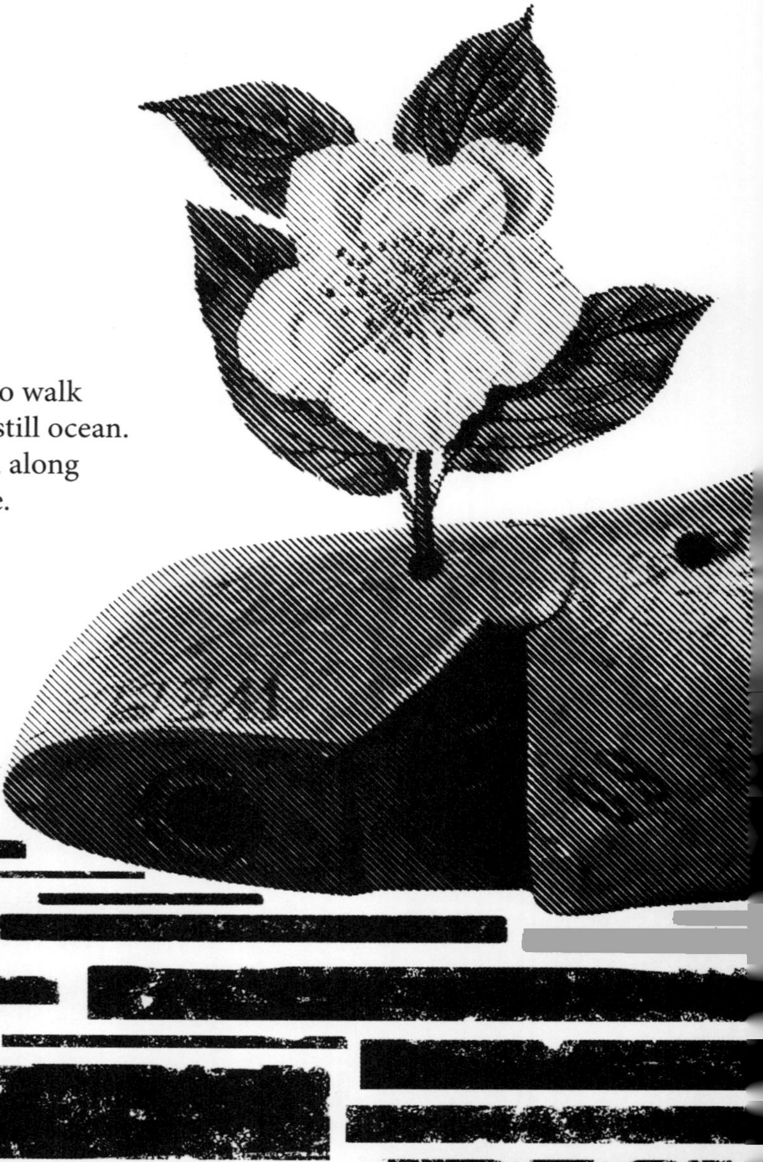

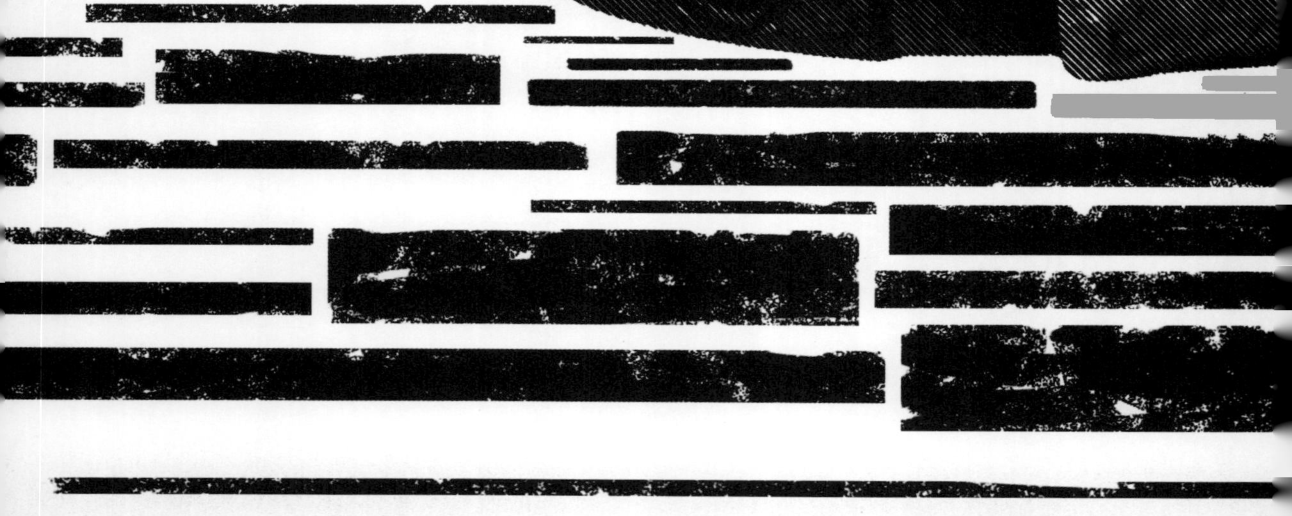

As we cross the cemetery,
I feel my mother's warm hand in
mine. I know that with this same
hand, she will open her drawer this
afternoon, will take out the letter
and read it, perhaps for the last time.

As we walk in silence, I feel in my other hand the hand my father used in the middle of the night to open the drawer and write what I watched him write.

That night, after leaving the study, I climbed the stairs and saw Papá sitting next to Mamá on their bed, as always. It was the first time Papá let me come close enough to look at the letter that began with "My beloved."

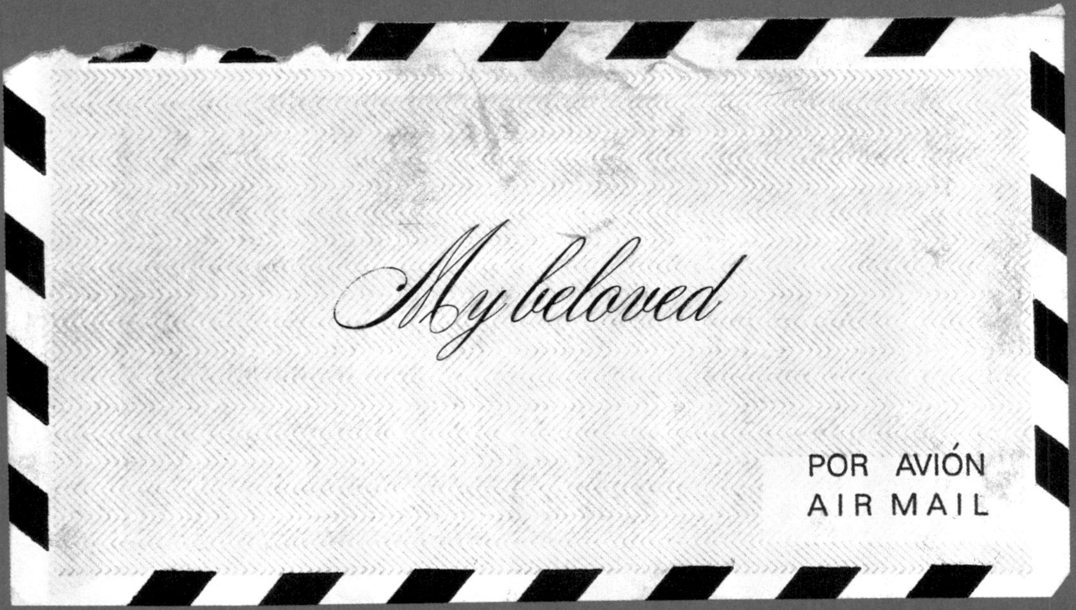
My beloved
POR AVIÓN
AIR MAIL

Not. That is what Papá had written.
He wrote it here and there, among
his own words of wind and sea,
as if he were a farmer scattering seeds.

        Not,

              not,

                  not.

I did NOT need to do it.
I did NOT kill our son.
I will NOT die now, my beloved

When the three of us reach the two white tombs, so like ships, I let go of my mother's hand.

"It's time to make peace," Papá tells me, as he heads into his tomb.

"Goodbye," is what I whisper, as I climb into my ship.

I say it with my mouth, and I say it by waving my hand, bidding farewell to my mother, but above all saying goodbye, goodbye forever, to the worst story in the world.

For the first time, Mamá doesn't cry.

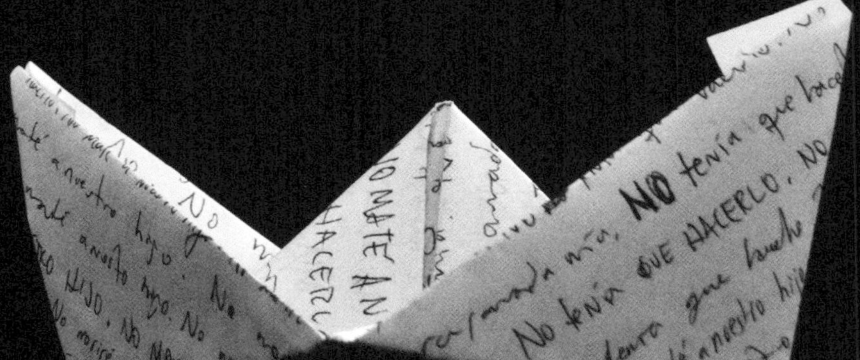
No tenía QUE HACERLO.